DEATH BY BEQUEST

by Mary McMullen

DEATH BY BEQUEST
A DANGEROUS FUNERAL
FUNNY, JONAS, YOU DON'T LOOK DEAD
THE PIMLICO PLOT
A COUNTRY KIND OF DEATH
THE DOOM CAMPAIGN
STRANGLEHOLD

DEATH BY BEQUEST

MARY MCMULLEN

PUBLISHED FOR THE CRIME CLUB BY
DOUBLEDAY & COMPANY, INC.
1977

All of the characters in this book
are fictitious and any resemblance
to actual persons, living or dead,
is purely coincidental.

ISBN: 0-385-12739-1
Library of Congress Catalog Card Number 76–50780
Copyright © 1977 by Doubleday & Company, Inc.
All Rights Reserved
Printed in the United States of America
First Edition

To my mother, Helen Reilly

DEATH BY BEQUEST

CHAPTER 1

It was between Trenton and Princeton Junction, on the train from Philadelphia to New York, that Waldo St. Clair conceived the idea of killing his wife.

Madness, at New Brunswick.

No, strangely possible by the time Elizabeth showed up, Elizabeth, New Jersey. And strangely necessary.

Not in this country, he decided while gazing upon the Jersey marshes and catching his first hazed distant view of the Chrysler Building and the Empire State. Too many people who knew her, knew them.

Especially Cy, Cyril Hall, his partner, although correctly that should be transposed, he thought. Let's face it, I work for him.

There was a long sit-still at Newark. A woman across the aisle from him was examining him closely, but Waldo was often studied with great interest by women and ordinarily it wouldn't have bothered him.

Did his new intentions show on his face? Was his idea written there for all the world to see?

He turned to the dirty window and the dim gray afternoon to try to catch an accurate reflection, but there was just the usual pair of black shadowed holes for eyes and the shine of his hair and a plane of cheek, smooth.

The train is being delayed, madam, because the police wish to pick up a passenger before we get to New York, an imaginary conductor said to the staring woman.

A heavy hand on his shoulder. Come along quietly, will you . . . ?

He was due for a semi-sabbatical. He—they—hadn't been

anywhere except Paris for a working week last year. And there was Mrs. Donahue, who wished to collect new young Irish painters—"Not the Lakes of Killarney, mind you, but something interesting, I'll leave it to you, Waldo dear . . ."

(And after all Celia could, in spite of present objections, decide to visit the house and see if there were family photographs, personal things she wanted.)

Yes, leave it to me.

Of course, things *might* straighten themselves out in some other way . . .

The train groaned and with a great wrenching shriek started again.

The wheel rhythm on the tracks agreed. Leave it to me leave it to me leave it to me.

"I'd appreciate it enormously if you would, Waldo," Celia had said, and then, "as long as you have to be in Philadelphia anyway. I wouldn't stick you with the job otherwise . . ."

Waldo had a low threshold of boredom and it was an understood thing that tedious but necessary family concerns would be attended to by Celia. She was peace-loving and had long ago accepted this very minor concomitant to being Mrs. Waldo St. Clair. They had been married for five years.

Waldo, for instance, had never been subjected to the tedium of a semi-annual afternoon tea visit at the house of her great-aunt in Philadelphia.

She had asked him to go with her, the first year, but he had already heard far too much about those frightful Pine Street afternoons to say yes.

"I'd love to, darling, but we're jammed, at the gallery, a good month, must lap it up while we may . . . and after all, for your sins, she's *your* aunt."

She got his message and after that didn't ask him again.

It was never with any hope of eventual material gain that she paid her visits. This never crossed her mind. Shortly before she died, her mother had said, "Do try to do your great-aunt twice a year, or at least once, I know she's a sore trial, but she's terribly lonely, friendless I think, and there are so few Gores to take tea with her . . ."

Abandon hope, all ye who enter here, Celia would think as she raised the knocker on the paneled white door and hesitated and then bravely dropped it. On a handsome brick block on upper Pine Street, of towering six-story fanlighted and shuttered houses, Laura Gore's was just vaguely shabby, and the white door was shockingly dirty.

"I dipped my fingers in the fireplace ashes and smudged the door myself, after dark, of course," Laura Gore had explained triumphantly, on one visit. "But this way, the house looking a bit tatty, they're not so likely to think I have color television to steal, or rubies. I've gotten four letters from my so-called neighbors about the door, and that broken shutter, but I just tore them up."

It was annoying to be made to wait to do something you didn't want to do at all, but there was always a pause of three or four minutes while Laura's ancient black maid, on command, climbed the great stairway to look from the second-floor landing down into the Philadelphia busybody to see who was mirrored at the door.

Then, "Oh, it's *you*, Miss Celia," as though the visit, and the time, hadn't been set forth clearly by letter; and as though her appearing here, to see her aunt, was close to an impossibility.

Through the looming ticking-covered cabinets and desk shapes—who needed three desks?—and across near-invisible old scatter rugs in the high broad hall, kept in almost total darkness, into what Laura referred to as her reception room. She saved on electricity and except in the case of a heavy dark rainfall, which seemed often to occur in the vicinity of her house, relied on the day outside for illumination.

Her aunt would be seen through the dusky yellow gloom— the discouraging color cast by old yellow damask curtains, stiffly pelmeted, and aging undercurtains of much-mended ecru Brussels lace—propped on her cane by the black marble fireplace.

A kiss on the paper-taffeta cheek. "I hardly know you, it's

been so long," in her aunt's grinding baritone. "You don't look well, have you been working too hard?—although of course people have forgotten the meaning of the word work—"

How could anyone look well in this mustard light, hemmed in and towered over by massive furniture the nature of which was only to be guessed at under the old-fashioned mattress ticking covers, now contributing their own share of dulled yellow between the stripes. Laura Gore kept only her wing chair, her tea table, and one guest chair uncovered. "Grease," she would say, "dust, rot, ants, chemical pollution—"

Celia had never been invited or was herself tempted to see the rest of the immense house, except for the bathroom at the top of the first flight of stairs, which had a tub encased in mahogany and cane, and crimson velvet flocked wallpaper. Beyond the bathroom were closed doors, darkness, another leap of stairs from the landing, a smell of dust and heavy soured hanging air.

"Try to find out," Waldo had once abjured her with a show of fleeting interest, "what she's worth, if anything. You never know."

She was a near-recluse, her great-niece gathered, except for the daily morning walk in all weathers down Pine Street to the Delaware River, a round trip of four miles. No great affluence could be guessed at from the tea she offered: thin slices of white bread and butter, ginger snaps, condensed milk for which she had a fancy, a small half-full sugar bowl, paper napkins. She always, for the ceremony, wore thin white cotton gloves. "You never know what you're touching. Dirt everywhere."

Tea poured, the tirade and the torture began.

You should be able to put up with it, dismiss it, just another of life's occasional trials.

But the old woman's hatreds, deep, bubbling, were like pus oozing from a suppurating wound.

The last President she had had any respect for was Calvin Coolidge. She went from past to present and back again, the stench of rage pouring out, saved up for release to the rare visitor.

She was impartial in her bitter contempt for all ethnic groups, all races, colors, and creeds other than her own, which was white, Scotch-Irish, and Presbyterian.

As for her countrymen, "nobodies, we're in the hands of a pack of nobodies."

There were places in her world where she savored "a taste of the Bomb, blot it out, I say, clean it up . . ."

And maddeningly, "Richard Nixon was a fine man minced up by the Red press, thrown to slavering dogs at his heels." Her eyes sly, defying and combative, as if underlining the fact that hers was the revenge of the very old, and that the young and strong had to consider her frailty.

There had been times, earlier, when Celia had been driven to hot protest but it was like holding a straight quiet match flame to a bonfire, and in any case Laura didn't listen, merely waited until the other voice stopped and picked herself up intact in midsentence.

She gave it up and pretended it was no worse than being, in conversational terms, at the dentist's or on an operating table without enough anesthesia. Hang on and bear it, sometime it would end.

Laura did not limit herself to social and political issues, but had plenty of curdled anger for near people, real people. She was particularly given to excoriating Celia's father, of whom Celia was very fond.

He had been a highly successful and style-setting magazine illustrator and was now retired and painting happily in Mexico.

"To think, dabbling away with his box of colors when his father had a place all ready for him in the law firm, but a lightweight, always a lightweight, no spine, no convictions, I hate people who think everything's funny, and you can't tell me his drinking didn't hasten your mother's death—

"Fortunate in a way your cousin by marriage, Bernard's mother Lottie, died in that car crash, she took after my own sister Jessica, sounded like her too, and Jessica ended up ranting and raving in a county home, my father was ashamed of her and didn't want any part of it, he changed the name when they put her in . . .

"How's your prancing husband Waldo? Lucky I met him at the wedding, first and last chance I've ever had to see him, looks like—it may sound old-fashioned to you, the word—a womanizer.

". . . well, your poor mother. The worst thing that ever happened to her, stop me if I'm repeating myself, was to meet your father."

Other people's deaths, and her own survival, excited her in an unpleasant manner. She herself was eighty-nine and looked every hour of it. Obituaries took at least one more lingering cup of tea, which by now tasted very brown and acid to her listener.

"Cancer of the bone marrow, she would have to come up with something unusual . . .

"His brandy caught up with him. Heart, and twenty years later than we all expected.

"Well, bless us, *she* died, and I had the feeling she was in her grave ten years ago, d'you suppose they've kept her around, embalmed?"

The room reeked of her ancient and ailing pug, who punctuated her monologue with an occasional sigh or groan, which could be interpreted as pain or agreement or overpowering boredom.

Celia would fight the desire of her eyelids to lower, close against the yellow light, blot out the room, the old woman, the dog, but the time she allotted for the visit was two and a half hours and she hewed gallantly to it.

Always, before she went, there was a special verbal blow delivered to the side of the head. Bernard, a cousin of what remove she had never been certain, was employed in this tactic of Laura's. Celia hadn't seen him since she was a child and even then her mother had murmured, "Be polite about it, but no, don't go off and play with Bernard, Celia, he's not . . . nice . . ."

"Well, once or twice a year is better than nothing I *suppose*,

Celia. Thank God for Bernard, he takes thought to a lonely old woman, I saw him in April and then again in June I think, and sometime later in the summer . . ."

She wondered if in turn her visits were multiplied and used as a stick to whack Bernard with.

At four-thirty, to catch the five o'clock New York Express from Thirtieth Street Station, she would make her farewells and flee down the marble steps, feeling scalded, used up, and with the weight of the world thrown on her shoulders.

Then, as the train approached New York, a lifting of depression, a feeling that there was, after all, cheer and warmth, work and laughter, even delight to be found . . .

Don't think of Great-aunt Laura, white-gloved against contamination, deep in hate, until next spring.

She was, however, given occasion to think again of Laura Gore late in October. Laura Gore died the death usually, in popular opinion, accorded to the virtuous and deserving: suddenly and without warning, in her sleep.

She left her house and all its contents, and the seven thousand dollars she had in the bank—"I'm afraid there are no stocks, no bonds, no other properties of any kind or description," the lawyer, a Mr. Prentice, had said disapprovingly—outright, to her great-niece Cecelia St. Clair.

Miss Gore had, he informed her, been living on the income of a trust left to her by her father, which after her death would revert absolutely to Pennsylvania Hospital. "Too bad," Mr. Prentice said. "A handsome sum of money, very handsome indeed. But I don't think there's a prayer of breaking it, not a prayer."

Celia went to the funeral, at which the devoted Bernard did not appear. Not that she would have known him; but there were only Vera, the old maid, four extremely old women, the minister, a Mr. Farquahar, and Prentice.

After returning from the cemetery, she dutifully saw to the dispensing of sherry for the ladies and whiskey for the gentlemen, along with Vera's shrimp sandwiches, hot triangular meat pastries, chocolate cake and coffee.

Alone for a moment, drinking her coffee, and impelled by combined fatigue and mild curiosity, she pulled up a box-pleated ticking corner and studied a small portion of what she considered a Jacobean monstrosity, originally stained black but greenish with mold, scorpions and bats and dead game, rabbits and birds, hung upside down. Most appropriate.

She was in time to catch the four-o'clock express.

Never again, that house, never, never again.

". . . as long as you have to be in Philadelphia anyway. I wouldn't stick you with the job otherwise."

Waldo's business in Philadelphia was concerned with the Freeman Galleries on Chestnut Street. There was an auction he was interested in, a man overtaken by market losses selling his collection of paintings of the Hudson River School, for which he had a client up his sleeve.

He took an early train and went first to the house on Pine Street, get it over with. Shabby or not, and Celia made it sound ghastly, it ought to be worth at least fifty, sixty, with luck seventy thousand dollars according to his information from friends who knew about things like real estate in Philadelphia.

It's not a house, it's a goddamned cliff, he thought, impressed in spite of the dirty white front door. He got out the key that Celia had given him, handed to her by Prentice, and let himself into the hall. It was a dark iron day in early December.

With no one around to worry about electricity bills and say him nay, he witched on lamps prodigally as he went. His nose knew something before his brain and wits did.

He ruthlessly snatched off ticking covers. Junk probably, but . . .

And what, he thought, stunned, to my wondering eyes do appear, but Beidermeyer, Louis XV and XVI, Hepplewhite and Chippendale, Chinese lacquers, shimmering mysteries of mother-of-pearl and fruitwood inlays, jasper and malachite and, Christ, that must be solid gold, those handles . . .

This was in the front hall alone. He looked down in the glare cast by the bronze dolphin lamp on the post of the balustrade and saw old silk Persian scatter rugs, a rose garden, a cage of birds, a flight of butterflies, a field of poppies, dim, trampled, but entirely retrievable.

Hardly trusting his shaking hand, he opened a red lacquer cabinet that looked to him to be seventeenth century, and saw in it the famille rose and famille verte vases, a willowware ewer so early as to be unmarked, a great blackened silver tureen, prehallmark, an immense glistening egg like the production of a giant robin—Fabergé? Yes, Fabergé. A girdle of gold and diamonds about its plump center—

He never made the auction at the Freeman Galleries. He went without midmorning coffee, without a midday drink or two, without lunch.

The first floor of the house held Laura Gore's reception room, dining room, library, immense kitchen and pantries. On the floor above were a sitting room and three bedrooms and two yawning bathrooms. There were four bedrooms and a bath on the floor above that, children's rooms and nursery on the next, and servants' rooms at the top.

The riches, the treasure, only stopped short at the children's floor, although even there, there were huge chests of toys that looked promisingly ancient. Not one of his fields of expertise; he must brush up on antique toys.

On some broad landing—he'd forgotten whether it was the second or third floor—he stopped and did something he couldn't remember having done since childhood.

He hugged himself in rapture, lower lip caught under his white upper teeth, breath held.

Another childhood emotion surfaced. If it was beyond dreams wonderful, it probably wasn't true.

There must be a catch, something staring him in the face, that in his delirious excitement he wasn't seeing at all.

He went down to the telephone under the stairway and called Prentice's office. Was there, he asked in a hurried bored voice, any inventory of the contents of Miss Gore's house? No, sorry, there wasn't—after leisurely investigation away from the phone, while his heart pounded painfully—or at least not on deposit at the law office.

Celia. A talented and successful designer of fabrics, her father an artist—how could she not sense the presence of gloriously beautiful things? But she had been brought up, she told him, in amiable bohemian clutter, her mother was a writer of children's books, nobody cared much about house-proud possessions and style.

And she had recalled the shrouding covers from early childhood; their deathliness had frightened her a little then. "That woman if she ever dies will leave a small fortune in striped cotton ticking." Besides, there was her hatred of the house and all its associations, the scalding aunt, the ailing pug, the bitter teaparties, which might have put blinders on her. Her only object, once having arrived, to get away, leave it behind, forget it—

All that aside, she was an open person, sometimes self-betrayingly transparent. No, she couldn't know. She didn't keep things from him, material things included. When sales were going badly at the gallery, as they occasionally inevitably did, there wasn't a problem of money. She owned their apartment; her father had given it to her as a present before she married, when he went off to Mexico. She made thirty thousand dollars a year as head designer at Titania Fabrics. They had a comfortable joint checking account, share and share alike, no questions asked or even thought of.

Replacing the covers, checking windows, locking up the house, he felt an immense weight of possession lying on him.

Thieves, vandals—the house empty—but then, there was no television set, color or otherwise, no stereo system, not even a radio, none of the usual quickly disposable snatch-and-grab. The kitchen cutlery was stainless steel; no doubt there was a mint's worth of old silver hidden in the drawers of the eighteenth-century breakfront in the dining room, but he hadn't been able to find a key.

Unusual security precautions undertaken right now might rouse suspicion or whet the appetites of the burglarious. Let it go, leave it to luck, until—

Until what?

Which must have been the first thread in the little skein that began to curl in and out of his thoughts, between Trenton and Princeton Junction.

CHAPTER 2

"Oh, Waldo, I can't," Celia said. "I mean, we can't, not at this time of the year, Christmas coming—"

He had anticipated this and was prepared to be gently persuasive, not arbitrary, demanding.

"What d'you mean, you can't," he said. "You're the crown jewels and the Queen of Sheba at Titania, and they know you'll design your way across the Atlantic and back anyway."

"But the gallery, this is one of your best seasons—"

The gallery was Hall and St. Clair, on Madison Avenue between Sixty-fifth and Sixty-sixth Street. Waldo, after working happily and well there for five years, had bought into it when his uncle Walter left him seventy-five thousand dollars. It had been opened in the twenties by Cy Hall's father and had simply been Hall and Son before Waldo wrote his check. He was surprised and pleased when Cy added his name in gold leaf on the window and over the door; it was by no means a full partnership he had paid for. He wondered later, nervously, if that meant Cy had plans of pulling out himself, sooner or later. Something not to think about, so don't. The dips and bad times notwithstanding, the gallery was a solid institution with a remarkably fine reputation.

"Nothing Cy can't handle, between chapters, or if he's otherwise occupied Irena's all over the place. As I've told you, she's a marvelous saleswoman."

It gave him a pleasant sense of daring to use her name so easily and casually, his tongue slipping lightly over the syllables, as if it was anyone's name. And to allow himself to say nice praising things about her to his wife.

They were in the living room of their apartment in a handsome brownstone in Chelsea. Cocktail hour in the day of an attractive New York couple. Celia, in copper silk pants and a black velveteen tunic, curled into the corner of a down cushioned sofa covered in one of her own linens, peacocks and zebras and unicorns in a lovely never-never landscape. Waldo, mixing their second martini and bending to prod his genial fire; in the expensive well-tailored French cotton pajamas, putty-colored tonight, that he liked to put on when he came home from work, and with his shapely feet bare.

A casserole of chicken, mushrooms, cream, tarragon, chestnuts, and chablis was in the oven, sending a soft promising smell into the living room. The tomatoes, stuffed with themselves and crumbled bread and sage and parsley and topped with Parmesan, were in the oven too. The round table in the corner, clothed floor-length in Celia's glistening Sun on Icicles chintz, was set, candles lit, peacefully striking sparks from crystal wineglasses and silver.

Before proposing the trip abroad, he had been telling her about the house.

"A few good things, I gather, I didn't take all that long—"

He watched her closely.

She seemed to have forgotten her drink and was staring into the fire and he thought he knew what, or whom, she was seeing there.

"Darling, pay attention, this is business, the house could bring in anything upward of fifty thousand or so, maybe a lot more."

"Oh, sorry, yes—and did you find anything at Freeman's?"

A good wife should interest herself in her husband's day; and should not be wandering down flowery lanes, although when it started there hadn't been flowers but the first sweet snow crystaling against their faces and the sheets of white wind caught in the streetlight . . .

"No," Waldo said. "Freeman's was a blank. I think we can leave putting the house on the market until after Christmas, or the New Year. They always drag their heels over probate anyway."

He went over to the window and looked out into the night. "Rain starting . . ." and then very slowly, his voice seeming to come from a distance, as if his mind too was somewhere else, "Perhaps you'd like to pull yourself together and pay one last visit there, go through it and see if there are family things you might want to keep . . ."

He turned around again and came and stood over her, the glass pitcher dangling from his hand.

She found his intent gaze, roving her face, a difficulty, and—horrible thought, how could she?—an intrusion. Drop it, leave it alone, the snow, the hand, the cut of his mouth, the feel of it. They were here, the two of them, Mr. and Mrs. St. Clair, and this was now.

"No, I won't at all want to go through it," she said. "That house is over. If you think there's anything valuable, or that *you* want, I'll leave it to you."

There was something about the arrangement of her body on the sofa, a melting grace, almost a voluptuousness, not quite Celia, that stirred an irrational jealousy in him.

"You're usually the one of us who copes, in your softhearted way," he said. "A huge houseful of furniture and odds and ends—God, do you know how many *pots* alone there are in the kitchen?—to sell or give or throw away— Am I really stuck with it? Is there no way out?"

Typical of Waldo to make what was admittedly a tedious chore sound like a matter of life or death.

"It's really finally your turn, Waldo," she said with a gentle stubbornness unusual in her. "It's our house, not just mine. Besides, you'd know what was worth selling and I wouldn't—I don't know a damned thing about furniture. And," with a lifting joy and gaiety, "I'm just about finished with this drink, may I have my other one?"

The joy paid for the darkness, the guilt; the guilt and longing and deep unhappiness in their turn paid back for the joy.

"Here it is, and here's to"—a hesitation, a plunge—"several

weeks on at least a semi-vacation, I have business in Ireland but we'll have plenty of romping time, I called Aer Lingus from Penn Station so I could hand you a surprise when I got home, we're leaving, let's see, a week from this coming Friday. So you've plenty of time."

And then her instant, "Oh, Waldo, I can't—"

He had discovered early in life that if you had any plan that might be considered even a little devious, the nearer you could stay to touchable truths the better.

"I'd hate to go without you," he said softly, "but in any case I'm going. Not only in pursuit of pictures but— You may or may not remember I have a trauma staring me in the face and I've got to get the hell into another atmosphere to get safely through it."

His fortieth birthday; the Sunday after next. She was thirty-three, but she knew that, perhaps even more so with men than with women, it was a bad, rough anniversary to hurdle. People no longer went around blithely agreeing that life begins at forty. Men did all sorts of wrenching things when they hit that particular beach: started love affairs, or divorced their wives, changed jobs or threw them up altogether and went off to Tahiti to paint or comb beaches. Thinking, this is the time, now or never, to shape the rest of my life. Stop drifting, start moving, do something, anything, head straight for what you've always wanted.

"You look ridiculously underage, Waldo dear," she said, and not only to comfort him. It was true.

Not tall, but so well proportioned you didn't realize it until he stood close to you: a hard, slim, graceful body. Olive skin stretched tight and fine across the broad upper face, the narrow lower one. Fashionably cut shining dark hair and sparkling brown eyes, the intriguing darkness and faintly piratical set of bone and mouth startlingly underlined by a deep dimple in his left cheek when he smiled.

There was no dimple now; he looked suddenly lost, her confident Waldo. Far away, beyond consolation. Desperate . . . ?

"I'm sorry," Celia said, "heaving your surprise back in your face like a wet snowball." She had wanted to add the word darling at the end of her sentence but it somehow got stuck in her throat. Endearments could only be used by her with absolute honesty.

He saw she was trying to move, emotionally, toward him, toward going away with him when she didn't want to, and he said, very quietly,

"It will be five years on New Year's Eve, for us. I thought it would be an especially good time to celebrate. And"—he paused, deliberately, sipping his drink, his gaze deep in hers— "renew our marriage vows. It never hurts to freshen them up."

She didn't dare look away, and was horrified to feel the flare of heat on her skin—did it show? And then she was hot all over, trying not to struggle, tremble, on the end of his pin. But that was nonsense, it was probably a perfectly normal, if for him rather extravagant, sentiment he had just expressed. Nothing clear, crisp, final had yet suggested itself to her; sometimes she thought it was all in her head.

Dear God, surely she hadn't murmured the name in her sleep?

But it worked, and they both knew the decision was now shared and made.

"Well, lovely, then," she said. "But Aer Lingus or no Aer Lingus, I've got to go and stir my chicken and see to the tomatoes."

It was a vital necessity to take herself and her face away from him for a few recovering moments. He bent and kissed her forehead. "Happy casserole, darling."

A good idea, looked at healthily. Get away from a distance and watch it shrink to size. Stare at yourself from the other side of the Atlantic, see the foolish lovesick woman in New York. She dwelt on the derisive words.

But alone in the kitchen, she went away again, very much against her will.

"Take a look if you can snatch a moment," Waldo said. "Marvelous but absolutely frightful if you know what I mean.

They all look to me like fresh chicken guts seen through a
heavy rain. Cruel and bloody, and romantic. They're selling
like mad."

Months before that, she had found herself in a corner at a
cocktail party with Cy Hall, whom she knew and didn't know;
they had been acquainted for five years. Waldo, to these semi-
strangers, was a convenient meeting place for conversation.

"Waldo is objective," Cy Hall said, peering into his scotch.
"He knows how to entrap owners of fleets of taxis, and towboat
tycoons. Whereas I'm subjective. I buy what I like and he buys
what *they* like."

Politely, intelligently, Celia answered, "But you couldn't
have stayed open, paying the rent, all these years, decades, by
being merely subjective? I don't know anything about fad and
fashion but I know what I like?"

He gave her his sudden wide charming smile. "It may sound
self-serving, but after a while, if you find you like things enormously, if they choose you instead of your choosing them, it
turns out a lot of other people will respond the same way."

"Like dowsing, the willow in your hand twitching when
you're over water, for your well?"

"Yes, a little."

It seemed to her as good a way as any to describe natural
taste without crassly laying claim to it.

She had gotten a different version from Waldo, long ago.
She remembered it because of the unexpected bitterness that
had lain under the words. Waldo had been in one of his dark
moods. She suspected that the source of them was that he had
wanted, badly, to be a painter and had thrown himself into it
and could never please his critical self with his work—"so I
became a peddler instead." About Cy, he said, "The grand sei-
gneur only buys what he thinks is good. He doesn't pander,
that's my department, that's why I'm valuable to him. It's a luxury he can allow himself."

Cy had money of his own, plenty of it, she gathered. And he
devoted the better part of his time at Hall and St. Clair to the
writing of biographies of artists. "Not art books," Waldo said.

"*Book* books." She had later read one, on Salvador Dali, and found it both witty and learned.

She thought, that night in early November, entering the long front room of the gallery and seeing him standing in a far corner beyond a moderate second-night crowd, that he probably didn't like the chicken guts. There were three exhibition rooms, going straight back in a line, to his office, and Waldo's, and Irena Tova's; this show occupied two of the galleries.

She saw his dour eye on a painting three feet away from him. Considering, fairly, giving it time; and then rejecting.

His expression amused her, and she smiled; and he saw her smiling and came over to her.

"Waldo's not here, if you've come to collect him, he was swept away by a woman who bought one of these things"—he gestured with a long fine hand—"ten feet by ten feet, to see how it would fit into her living room."

"That's all right, I just wanted a quick look around, they're ghastly, aren't they. Or"—in her soft modest way—"at least, I think."

"Will you have a glass of champagne? They're going so well that the bar's open a second night."

"No thank you, I must run." She didn't tell him the reason why, it would sound childish. The first snow of the year had started coming down as she left her office and now was whirling thickly on the wind. She couldn't wait to get out into it, and walk.

"Then just a minute till I get my coat, I was going to leave too about now."

As they waited at the corner of Madison and Sixty-sixth for the light to change, wind whipping them, tiny dry snowflakes bouncing off the surface of her big round glasses, he sensed her euphoria, her joy.

"Do you like the snow?"

"I love it. I know what the streets will turn into, but, this first snow, I'm always mentally putting on my mittens and getting out my Flexible Flyer."

He laughed. "Think of the poor commuters in their cars

cursing all the way to Westport, or Tarrytown—I love it too. Here, give me your hand," as the light changed to green and a tide of cars turning in from the side street did battle with them in their attempt to cross.

Cy swore under his breath at a cab driver who out-maneuvered them in the middle of the street, a sort of Manhattan Russian roulette, nerve against nerve, man against wheels, vulnerable flesh against metal.

She had forgotten to put her gloves on and his hand was bare and warm. Palm to palm, something happened between their hands.

He linked his fingers firmly through hers—how long could they have been standing, trapped, in the middle of Madison Avenue?—and then got her safely to the west side of the street.

They paused under the streetlight, astonished eyes meeting, his head bent, hers raised to the snow and to him.

"Celia." As though formally identifying her.

"Is it . . . Cyrus or Cyril? I've wondered."

"Cyril. I got hell for that in school."

Lit theatrically from above, he was larger and realer than life. Long strong shadowed cavalier's face with a slight crookedness that was endearing, warm crystal gray eyes examining, but no, not real, unreal.

Thick hair a mixture of fair, red, and gray, brushed straight across a broad thoughtful forehead, snow clinging to the hair now and starring his heavy eyebrows. An unworked-at elegance about him, carriage, clothes, demeanor.

Thirty-eight, Waldo had said. He looked older, seasoned. The mouth, so close, was both male and tender, and a little ascetic, or was it a mouth showing his spirit, his secrets? Not fair to study it from six inches away and wonder . . .

His wife had died of leukemia four years ago. Waldo said that he had adored her. Awful to think of this man, this stranger—no, not a stranger, they'd been saying hello, how are you, to each other for years—losing someone he loved.

He moved forward and kissed her lightly and warmly on her mouth. One arm was around her.

"Don't worry," he murmured consolingly, "people will think we're old friends parting—everybody kisses everybody these days. Or husband and wife going their different ways before they meet again at home—"

She felt he was talking to cover up some suddenly yawning gulf, some bewilderment as deep as her own.

Following his proposed script, he held her close against his English trenchcoat, something underneath, a big, tall, agile, powerful man.

He kissed her again, in open possession, and said cheerfully, intimately, very audibly (they were after all being looked at in spite of his "everybody kisses everybody these days") and in retrospect unbearably,

"I may be home a little late, I think I'd rather have veal chops than steak, and seeing you like this weather so much you can take your turn to walk the dog."

Coming from quiet composed Cy Hall, it sounded like mild hysteria, or drunkenness, but she thought he was quite sober as far as alcohol went.

She made a reluctant pulling-away motion and he immediately dropped his arms.

"*I'll* be home a little late if I don't . . ."

"Let's see, you're downtown and I'm going uptown, I'll get you a cab—" his face curiously flushed, or maybe it was the reflection of the light turning red near them. Before she had time to frame a proper good night—and in any case what would that consist of?—he was opening a yellow door and handing her in.

"Good night, Celia." He at least did it properly. "Enjoy it while it lasts, the snow," and with a wave at her window as her cab pulled away, he was behind her, gone, in the first magical snowfall of the year.

CHAPTER 3

When Bernard Caldwell saw the death notice in the New York Times, called Laura Gore's lawyer and found that he had not been so much as mentioned in her will, he allowed himself one of his rages.

Sometimes they cost him his job. He was a good salesman, enthusiastic, persuasive; impervious to everyday resistance and even insult. He had sold farm equipment, chemicals, vitamins, motorboats, and cosmetics among other things, always working for large manufacturers.

But there came a moment in each of the many jobs when the elastic band would stretch too far, and snap.

He was skilled at writing objective-sounding references for himself. He made friends easily and always gave the name of a reliable buddy at his last job, in case his new employer wanted to check.

The rages had cost him a wife and after her a blonde and a redhead.

But there was no one to see him now, in the small bungalow he rented outside Trenton, New Jersey, where he currently worked for Brinner Brothers, Everything for Bowling.

I suppose it's because of that time in August I said something, making a kind of joke about it, to the old hag, the sneaking old bitch, about hoping she wouldn't forget me in her will —suddenly remembering the harsh indrawn breath, the needle glare of her eye—was his last coherent thought before he deliberately let himself go.

He picked up the desk chair and smashed it against a window. Glass went crashing and two legs of the chair snapped off.

He ripped the spread from the bed and—gratifying surge of muscular power—tore it in half. He hurled a heavy glass ashtray at the kitchen door. It made a pleasing dent in the painted wood before it showered in fragments back over his feet. Don't scream, don't shout, someone in a passing car might hear him, even though his throat was bursting. He kicked the wastebasket and it shot across the rug dumping paper crumples and cigarette butts and ashes. Panting now, and beginning to tremble, he threw himself on the bed and stared at the ceiling.

All those visits, all those years. The stinking dog, the dark house with everything covered up, the tea when he would have given his right arm for whiskey, the gray steak and boiled potatoes for dinner, the shrill rasping voice going on, and on . . .

"Don't neglect your great-cousin, or whatever the hell she is," had been his father's advice to him. "Money there somewhere, I can smell it, even with the tacky way she lives, and as far as I know there's only one other cousin, somewhere around your age—"

He had visited her three, four times a year for more years than he cared to count. Grin and bear it, he'd say to himself, it's an investment . . .

There's only one other cousin somewhere about your age.

One other. One other. Not a mob of relatives standing in line before him, between him and her, in case anything should . . .

"A Mrs. St. Clair," Prentice had informed him. "Her great-niece."

He dredged about in his memory and found her dimly: a small girl, timid, who brought out what he thought of as the mischief in him, the arm seized and twisted behind her back, the startled scream of pain, her mother coming running, "Aw, we were only teasing each other, she pinched me first . . ."

He lay on his bed, daydreaming.

A soft kind of kid she had been, Celia, yes that was her name, Celia. Maybe she was still that way. "Certainly, Bernard, I see your point, it's only fair," he heard her saying.

That house. If the front door was scrubbed up, the broken

shutter replaced, those terrible old yellow darned lace curtains taken down—after all, it was a good block, the Gore house the only mild blemish on it—it should be worth at least sixty thousand dollars, maybe a hell of a lot more.

Daydreaming got you nowhere. He hadn't daydreamed the sale yesterday of six new bowling alleys to Trenton Fun and Games. He had gone out and made it.

Too bad the desk chair was broken. He dragged over a side chair and sat down at the desk in front of his portable typewriter.

Casting his eye about the room in search of the right approach, he noted the broken window and decided he'd call the police and say the house had been vandalized while he'd been away. That would square it with the landlord, he'd have to reglaze the window, it was a medium-to-bad neighborhood, you had to expect this kind of thing on this kind of street.

Mrs. Waldo St. Clair. It sounded odd, rich; she probably had money, or her husband did, and the bitch wouldn't even need it.

He'd get her address from that voice-down-the-nose lawyer.

This is for starters, he thought, feeling active, brisk, and reassuringly in command of himself again.

Just for starters.

"Dear Cousin Celia," he began, "I don't know if you remember me, but" . . .

"I've had a most peculiar letter about that house," Celia told Waldo. "Somewhere between a whine and a threat and a handshake from the past. From a, I suppose he's some kind of cousin, a man named Bernard."

Waldo, lazy at his end of the sofa, snapped very delicately to attention.

Ordinarily, when informed about letters she got, he would say, "In a sentence, please," to spare himself any remote possibility of boredom.

She waited for this request and instead he said, "What do you mean by some kind of cousin?"

"Well, let's see." She really wasn't concentrating. She was somewhere else, again.

Waldo wondered impatiently if she had any idea of what had happened to her face, the pearliness that had come over it, the wash of beauty he had never seen before.

Not that she wasn't nice-looking in her quiet way, soft-speaking brown eyes behind the solemn horn-rimmed glasses, dark witty eyebrows eloquent too, under a grave forehead. Loosely falling brown hair cut in a bell, silk-fresh and clean, looking as if a light wind had just passed through it, a short straight nose, an amiable intelligent mouth, very fair skin which seemed almost blue when she was tired and was a dead giveaway, the color catching it, when she was embarrassed or happy.

Or in love.

When *they* had first been in love, he had said, "You come on misleadingly like a mouse. But then you turn into a wind-chime in a breeze, you hear—you notice—one faraway delightful thing after another, your voice, your eyes . . . and that funny spilled-out laugh of yours . . ."

She closed her eyes; partly to summon up Bernard and partly to avoid Waldo's piercing glance.

"Laura was my grandmother's sister. Bernard's grandmother was Laura's own first cousin. That would make Bernard her first cousin three times removed and he'd be my . . ." She paused.

"Second cousin, the hell with the removes," Waldo said. "Where's the letter, I'd like to see it."

She got up obediently and went to the straw wastebasket beside the desk and took out the letter and the envelope, shaking ashes from them.

"Dear Cousin Celia, I don't know if you remember me but we met as kids in what I jokingly used to call her, and she lapped it up, Great-cousin Laura's house on Pine Street. *Great cousin*, get it? Seems now there are only two survivors of that once mighty clan left in the whole wide world, and that's you and me. She spoke of you very nicely, appreciated your visits, I can imagine what they cost you in time and patience, I know

what they cost me, God! She was in some kind of a bad mood
when I went to see her in August, and well you know how they
are at that age, she must have done something or other to her
will, she'd told me often I'd be well remembered in it, and now
the old doll wipes me right off the slate. I know you'll agree
how unfair that is, it isn't as if there's a whole crew waiting
around to put their fingers in the pot, there's just as I said you
and I. I'm prepared to be reasonable if you are. I'm in Trenton, two drinks away on the Penn Central from your town, and
will be available for a friendly talk at any time. Hoping you'll
see that this is the only fair thing and that you'll get in touch
with me immediately if not sooner, and with recollections of
what a nice little soft-hearted kid I remember you as, Yours,
Bernard." Under his written signature, as a memory freshener,
was typed his full name, Bernard Caldwell, 1010 Voss Road,
Trenton, New Jersey, and his telephone number.

Waldo's silence puzzled her. "Are you thinking we ought to
give him some money, five thousand, ten, when the house is
sold?"

"Not at all, he hasn't an earthly claim to it, the will is cut
and dried, no loopholes, and you say she was sane when you
last saw her . . ."

"As sane as she ever was," Celia said.

"What does he look like, this Bernard?"

"Why . . . ?"

"For God's sake, Celia, don't you get the cheery threat in
the 'only two survivors' and then he says it again? Don't you
think it would help if you met him somewhere in a dark alley
—to know what the other survivor looked like?" He added,
"He probably doesn't know yet if you're safely married, or
divorced, widowed, alone . . ."

She couldn't tell him that the letter had just barely floated
over the level of her consciousness; that there were other
things, troubling delightful things, obsessing her, crowding everything else out. She had merely noted down his name and address in her little green leather book and vaguely decided to

talk it over with Waldo; Bernard's claim seemed reasonable enough.

Now she forced clarity and concentration on herself.

"I have no idea what he looks like. The last time I saw him was when I was eight and he was ten. He said, Let's both of us go upstairs and take all our clothes off, and I said no, and he twisted my arm behind my back and hurt me horribly, I still remember it . . . fair-haired, though it could have turned dark or gray since then, nothing particular to notice about his face . . ."

"I'll answer the letter," Waldo said. "I'll just tell him politely to go screw himself. Two can play at the iron hand gambit, and my velvet glove will be of better quality than his. And" —he gave her an odd smile—"I'm glad you started early in life, refusing improper invitations from the other sex, Celia."

It is impossible to fall in love while crossing Madison Avenue, in the snow, in a snarl of taxis, holding a hand.

She assured herself of this many times the following day.

The morning after that, Cy Hall called her, at eleven. She was at work, at her drawing board. He was in her neighborhood, he said, and could he take her to lunch? Easy and casual.

Maybe he was trying to clear up impossibilities too. She said without fuss or hesitation that she would like to, and met him at a small pink-lit Italian restaurant three blocks from her office.

He was at the bar. He came instantly to her and looked hard at her face, eyes moving over every inch of it, reminding her of his saying her name, quietly and clearly, identifying her, under the streetlight.

"I have a table, unless you'd rather have a drink at the bar first . . . no? Give me your coat . . ." He checked it, pocketed the tab, lightly took her arm and moved her through the crowded buzzing room to a table in the corner where they sat side by side on tufted black vinyl.

He had a way, Celia noticed even that early, of attracting fast and attentive service. "Martini?"

"I'm better off with scotch in the middle of the day . . ."

To the waiter, "One dry martini, one scotch, bring the water on the side," and then without any kind of throat-clearing or any change of expression, and in a perfectly natural way, took her hand where it lay on the tufted vinyl and closed his over it.

Their drinks came. He kept her hand, managing his cigarette, lighter, and drink with his left.

The public face, the private hand. She felt herself slipping, already almost lost; she had been going to be brisk, conversational, a new friend made, there were lots of things she could talk about with him, the gallery, painting in general of which she had garnered a lot from Waldo and had ideas about herself—

At first they talked very little, but looked at each other.

"It's hell having all these people around," he said. "Does my face look strange?" almost anxiously.

No, it looks marvelous, although too close . . .

"No . . . Does mine?"

"Yes. Or maybe in all these years I never really looked at you before. Do you always go around with all ten wicks in your candelabra lighted?"

That did it.

She began to talk, too fast, in her well-informed soft intelligent way, about the lawsuit of the Rothko estate against the Marlborough Gallery. He ordered a second drink, listening eyes on her, not necessarily her voice but her face, her own eyes.

"I suppose in a way it's a landmark kind of case—" Do go on talking.

She looked and tried not to be seen doing so at his showing hand, the immaculate nails somewhere nicely between almond and square, the long fingers, the lightly growing reddish fair hair on the back of the hand, he must have been as a little boy an enchanting strawberry blond. Thin plain everyday watch, not showoff, no built-in calendar or eerie huge lighted nu-

merals. Crisp half-inch of pale yellow Oxford cloth cuff showing under the sleeve of his dark gray suit, simple square amber
cufflink.

The eyes, mountainy, somewhere between gray and blue in
this light—

People fall in love with their eyes. Look away.

Love is recognition, perhaps the highest form of it.

You.

Look away again.

" . . . and, what will it do to the good faith of other galleries
. . . ?"

"Yes," he said, as if adeptly fielding a conversational point
tossed to him. There was a faint thoughtful amusement at the
corners of his mouth. "While you keep the ball in the air, I'm
down here on earth. In a way, that is. To think . . . I've been
to your apartment for dinner. You collect shells. You've been—
you and Waldo—to mine. You once had coffee in my office on
a cold morning when you couldn't get a cab and came in to
warm up. I was invited over one Sunday to your place on Fire
Island. You'd gotten sunburned and had to go to bed and
Waldo and I and some girl I brought with me had dinner without you, he cooked spaghetti and scorched it, he was burned
too and had had a pot of martinis—"

Thinking and not thinking about the possible reason for it,
she had dressed very carefully that morning. A soft wool in a
remote blue, scarved gracefully around her throat, pearls tangled carelessly in the scarf, pearls dangling from her ears.

Waldo watched her from the bed. He went in late most
days, ten o'clock or so. "People don't part with thousands
before lunch, usually."

He said, "Turn around, I'll be your mirror. You don't use
blusher as a regular thing, do you?—you've got a bit too much
on." She wielded a paper tissue. "There, you're ready for anything."

He gave her her first recognizable pang of guilt.

Cy watched her face as, remembering Waldo's voice, from
his pillows, she distractedly tucked back one swath of brown

silk hair behind a fine small ear. The other swath flew and shone and feathered against her cheek whenever she moved her head.

The moules à la marinière arrived.

She said timidly, "I think I'll need my hand—"

"You're perfectly welcome to it for the time being—"

He added severely, "Whatever that is, narcissus or something, that you have on, it tends to interfere with the wine and garlic." And a moment later, as he caught her staring at the tablecloth, so far buried in him that she had almost forgotten who she was and who Waldo was, "Pick up your fork, do. I'll race you to see who can finish the bowl first. And, if you insist on being social"—head tilted close to hers, and to hell with the watching eyes, people enjoyed watching lovers—"tell me in your madrigal voice, all about the fabric designing business."

Under the green canopy, as they lingeringly searched for farewells that could be said in daylight, with people passing, buses accelerating, taxis racketing, he said, "The idea that I have to say goodbye to you is outrageous."

"Say goodbye . . . ?" Voice so low he could hardly hear her.

"I mean, for now, for today."

It shouldn't have made her happy; it could be trouble, enormous trouble shaping up, shaking them all to the roots. Since marrying Waldo, she had not had a love affair or anything approaching it. But just this one afternoon, just for a few hours, she thought, I'll let myself be this happy.

When he called her at five o'clock she began to try, if feebly, to fight it.

"Have you finished up your butterflies, Celia?" A design she was working on that she'd told him about at lunch.

"Yes . . . no . . . almost— Cy, I think we should probably not talk at all, on the phone or anywhere, and not see each other for a week . . . that is, if you were going to . . ." Wretched pause, maybe this was all one-sided and he would think her mad, interpreting their hand-holding lunch as something of profound importance.

Everybody kisses everybody these days.

"You know that's absolute nonsense," he said.

She could see him at his desk in the big handsome office, the walls jammed with pictures, his typing table at right angles to his desk, the Persian rug, smoke blue and amber, the books, the easel in the corner, the glass and metal tea cart beside it from which he leisurely dispensed, in this inner sanctum, sherry and gin and whiskey while canvases on the easel were studied.

And Waldo in the next office, a smaller room, although he seldom stayed out there, but restlessly roamed the exhibition rooms, or pursued pictures and sculpture to far-ranging studios and lofts—but if he was there, Cy would be very sure to have his own door closed so he couldn't be heard, after all he'd said her name, openly and warmly.

She felt a prickle of discomfort.

"No, I mean it, if not for you then for me, I need it—I'm not used to whirlwind things like this, although they may be part of your everyday week—"

How bitchy that sounded, and all she had meant to do was let him know that she knew there might really be nothing in this to be taken seriously.

There was a pause, and then he sighed, and made a sound that could have been a faint laugh. "All right, Celia, I have to go to London anyway for a few days, I wanted to see you at least once before I left, but—" And then firmly, "Good night."

Even that early, he was tempted to tell her about Waldo and Irena Tova. Without his having any particular interest in the matter, it seemed fairly clear, the pairing. But he hated to be the one to administer the hard chop with the edge of the palm to the back of the vulnerable neck, under that sliding shining hair.

"But of course you didn't know. The wife is always the last to . . ."

CHAPTER 4

There was a fury about Waldo's lovemaking that both dismayed and pleased Irena Tova.

As so often in the past six months, they had a lazy lunch in a small French restaurant a few blocks from her apartment, wine and omelet and fruit and cheese, and then went home and to bed. They would turn up at slightly different times from slightly different directions, later, at the gallery, both of them shining and contented.

There wasn't much contentment in the sparkling little green and white bedroom today.

Irena sat up, stretched, and went pink and naked into the bathroom. He studied her sturdiness, the waist not at all narrow, breasts deep and firm. In a world of dieting women, she was slightly and he thought deliciously overweight, and perfectly happy about it.

"The thing about you, Irena," he would tell her, "is that you're somewhere between a worldly kind of girl, a hausfrau, and a comfortable old-fashioned whore."

Aware that he was leaving out the fourth Irena, tough, ambitious, acquisitive.

Cy Hall had hired her. Her father was a good friend and client of his. She had just gone through an unhappy divorce and wanted to work, get out into the world and breathe, she said.

She had started at Hall and St. Clair as a sort of girl Friday, fetching coffee, watering plants, taking dictation and typing letters. After a while she had been allowed to try her hand at a little selling, and then a little modest buying. She knew the field and loved it; and soon from her mysterious international background came friends with money to spend, friends with pictures worth displaying. She was now solidly entrenched.

As far as Waldo could gather, whe was a mixture of Hungarian, Dutch, and Jewish. Her father didn't believe in lazy young ladies lying about eating chocolates or worse still drinking early martinis; the allowance he gave her was lean and she worked not only because she wanted to but because she must. He was married to his second wife, twenty years younger than he, so the prospects in that direction were not promising. Added to which Irena's stepmother detested Irena.

Waldo felt for her something he couldn't quite define; he thought her as necessary to him as his heartbeat.

And she had told him, in the faint accent that charmed male visitors to the gallery, "Don't let it go to your head, Waldo, but you suit me. You really suit me." She pronounced the *w* in his name somewhere between an *f* and a *v*.

Rosier still from her bath, and shedding a faint mist of sandalwood-smelling powder, she came back into the bedroom, composedly put on her pale green chemise slip deep in ivory lace, and prepared to ease her feet and short hard shapely legs into her pantyhose.

"Come now," she said. "Not that man this morning, Bloomgarden? I think he'll be back this afternoon, I think he wants the Marisol, if Cy can be persuaded to part with it—"

The first several weeks at work, she had tried, with Cy, but sensed a closed door at the end of that particular inviting corridor and turned her attentions to Waldo.

"Are you going to collect your personal commission, in this bed, tonight? I heard him muttering to you, about dinner—"

"Look, as far as finances go, we're penniless orphans, adrift." Her penniless orphan's condominium apartment had been paid for by her father but the stiff maintenance was up to her. "Who was the man who said, We live not as we will but as we must? Work is work, Waldo, I don't drive myself into a fury when one of your ladies looks sheets and mattresses at you."

She had a round face, the fair skin transparent, shimmering, and slightly protuberant very dark blue eyes. Her hair was a child's natural soft gold, cut childishly short and curving in wings almost up to the corners of her eyes. She had a sensuous plump mouth, rosy on its own, and small sparkling white teeth. She exuded health and strength and always looked as if she had just stepped out of a sauna; and to underline the deliberate sexiness there was a fascinating suggestion of snowy apron, forearms floured as delightful things were baked, fragrance from her kitchen and from her freshly decanted wine.

To his silence, she went on, "And you go home to your Celia every night, don't you? And I assume when you're in the mood you fulfill your husbandly obligations? We've been over it and over it—by the way, get up, darling, and take your shower, and I'll fix coffee, it's getting on—" with a glance at her diamond watch, the source of which he had furiously wondered about.

"Yes, over it and over it. Penniless orphans, as you say. And, also as you say, if we said the hell with it and married, or at least arranged to have every day all day and every night together, she would hardly extend the benefits of a steady salary to the two of us, not just me—" He stared blackly in front of him. "Even if I yanked out what's left of my stake in the gallery it wouldn't last us a year and then what, and where, and how . . ."

"And neither of us fancies canned tomato soup, and instant coffee, and darning, whatever darning is. Yes, well then, no more sulks."

She went over and kissed him. A vital warmth and sustenance came from her. "And stop glaring and worrying. I'm perfectly satisfied with the way we are, for the moment."

For the moment.

He showered savagely, and then for the first time since they had become lovers he thought, Watch it, I'll have to step carefully here, no point in starting her wondering where we're heading, what's really in this for her, and is she wasting valuable time when she could be building some kind of nice little empire for herself? She was twenty-nine. A great deal of money walked in through the doors of Hall and St. Clair.

He came into the kitchen glowing and smiling from his

shower, brushed and groomed, in his beautifully cut loden cloth suit and creamy challis shirt and deep green woolen tie polka-dotted in simmering red, noticeable but like everything else Waldo wore right.

She always, just before they left the apartment, gave them hot fresh coffee, the best he had ever tasted, and little glasses of brandy.

"There's my own pristine Waldo back again. All right now?"

"Marvelous." He gave her his merry smile. "For the moment."

On the way downtown in the cab—"Drop me at Bergdorf's, there was a gray thing in the window I must have, gray and white ostrich feathers at the hem, chiffon I think"—he said, "You'll take a rain check for tomorrow? I have to go to Philadelphia to an auction, and oh yes, to see about a house somebody's left to Celia."

No point in driving too fast from Trenton to New York, although he badly wanted to, in his anger and excitement; he might get picked up by the bloody police.

Phrases from Waldo St. Clair's smooth, firm letter rang in his head. ". . . feel for you in your disappointment after your attentions to a distant relative, or your great-cousin, as you affectionately called her . . . must recall that the word Will is literally the will and wish of any given person as to the disposal of his or her property to the person he or she chooses . . ."

Affectionately. The slick bastard. It would be nice to know, necessary to know, what they looked like, what if any their soft spots were.

You didn't get to be a successful, well, in his own way, successful salesman without a bottomless well of persistence.

Hard-nosed, that's what I am, Bernard reminded himself.

He had no intention of taking the case to court, even with some contingency-style shyster lawyer. He hadn't enough to go on; Celia St. Clair was, as far as blood ties went, the closer of them to Laura Gore, and they'd always favor a woman. And

the old fool was as sane as she knew how to be when he'd seen
her in August, it was just that half-joke about her will that had
kicked over the applecart. Implying she might someday die.
Contingency or not, he had a feeling that if he lost a thin case
it would cost him money somehow or other, which he couldn't
afford.

But there were other ways, for a man free to come and go.

He stopped at a bar on the New York side of the Lincoln
Tunnel and had several whiskies. Planning, as he downed the
second, not a real rage of his, this first time, but just to show
that he was not a man to be taken lightly.

Cy Hall was standing in front of a large sunlit blue and
white Hopper talking to an elegant bent old woman in sables
when Bernard flung open the brass-embroidered beveled glass
front door of Hall and St. Clair.

Something about his clothes and his carriage convinced Bernard that this must be his man. He strode across the white
marble floor and rudely joined the two.

"Waldo St. Clair, is it?"

The woman in sables stared haughtily at the big heavy-shoul-
dered man in the slightly soiled raincoat and rakish broad-
brimmed black hat. He had a square overfed and overwhiskied
face, hard blue eyes under hard derisive black eyebrows that
met in the middle, and a nose that had once been good, bold,
high-bridged, broken in a bar battle many years ago and not
quite properly reset. It was at once an advantage and a disad-
vantage to him that he looked like and could have been so
many other men.

"No, it is not," Cy Hall said calmly.

This could be one of Waldo's artists—he didn't recognize
him, offhand—out for his blood, wanting to fight about prices,
and presumably up to and including with his fists, to judge
from his belligerent glare.

"Two rooms back, office door to the left, his name's on it."

He listened with one ear to Mrs. Wilberforce's hesitations,
"I *think* I'm sure but I'd like to *know* I'm sure, dear Cy . . .

tell me once again about its being an investment, and I know you tell me the truth, you've never misled me all these years except perhaps once, that Albers, John simply hated it and . . . oh yes, I remember now, I did sell it for seven hundred more than I paid you for it . . ."

With the other ear, he heard Waldo's light crisp step on the marble floor of the room beyond; he must have intercepted the raincoated man. Cy hoped that in case he wasn't a maddened artist he hadn't come in to rifle the safe. Not that there was much in it in the way of cash, mostly small and priceless pictures, and he didn't look like an art connoisseur . . .

But he did look distinctly and deliberately threatening.

However, you never could tell in this business. Last year about this time he had sold off the wall—or more accurately, accepted for confirmation the Fifth Avenue Bank check—a Franz Kline for $150,000 to a pale bald man in soiled sneakers and mended knitted string gloves who turned out upon later examination to be one of the Schuilthuises of Amsterdam and Southampton. The check was perfectly good.

The off-duty ear heard accurately, Waldo's "I was just on my way out, sorry," and the other man, loud, harsh, "Well, first round, right? *You're* St. Clair. You write a hell of a letter, worse than any lawyer."

There was no one else in the gallery besides the four of them.

At the sight of Waldo, his cousin Celia's husband—got it right this time—there had been a kind of sudden red haze behind his eyes.

College he hadn't made, because his old man committed suicide, so he'd been on his own early, knowing that he had something good, something not used, that had been strangled, stifled, when he went to work as a salesman—

And here was this immaculate man, his age, but in perfect shape, Racquet Club, he supposed, and a sailboat, maybe, in summer, terrific clothes in a played-down way, amused waiting eyes.

"What do you mean, first round? You make it sound like some sort of fight and I'd thought there weren't even grounds for an argument. If I take your meaning correctly . . . Bernard —may I?"

The haze got redder; something took over and he lifted his foot and there was a crash as a six-foot by eight-foot Hans Hoffman was kicked off the wall.

Mrs. Wilberforce, charmed by what sounded like excitement, stayed close to Cy's side as he strode into the middle room.

"What the hell is all this?"

Waldo, pale, was getting up the painting off the floor, first things first, as though the big man with the balled fists a few feet from him didn't exist.

Upon close examination, "It's okay, I think—the police, do you suppose?"

"Police nothing," Bernard said. "I slipped on your bloody polished marble floor and just managed to save myself. I could have had a bad fall. You'd have been hearing from my insurance people. And if you think this is the end of it, it isn't, it's just the beginning, Mr. Waldo your honor St. Clair."

He turned and walked very fast out of the gallery.

"Who," Mrs. Wilberforce asked breathlessly, "was that?"

"A cousin, distant thank God, of," he looked at her and not at Cy, "my own dear wife's."

He studied the canvas, restored to its place on the wall, inch by inch, muttered, "Oh Christ!" and then, "No, it's only a bit of cigarette ash," taking his handkerchief to it.

He added in a characteristic throwaway fashion, "Celia inherited a bit of propeerty in Philadelphia. He thinks he should have it. He reminded her on paper that there were only the two of them. I hope he doesn't carry a gun in that sagging raincoat." At a shrilling from the far end of the gallery, "My phone, I think."

"It might be a good idea to call your . . . own dear wife and tell her her violent distant cousin's in town," Cy said casually.

"Come along, Amy, and let me continue singing my song to you."

Bernard knew where Celia worked. Laura Gore, telling him about her loving frequent visits, and how talented, how successful her great-niece was, had compared Titania Fabrics favorably with Schumacher. "And as much as thirty, forty dollars a yard, fancy that!"

Waldo had called Celia. "Your thug cousin may be on his way to see you. Don't give an inch. And if I were you I'd take cover behind my drawing board and have a T-square at the ready. He's a rough customer."

They were both a little intimidated, she by his sudden looming in the doorway after the receptionist had notified her, he by the very female yet professional atmosphere, the orderly clutter and personal fragrance of her studio-office, color everywhere, the large businesslike drawing board facing him where, seated, she looked smaller than she was, and in some way barricaded against him.

He had had several more whiskies to calm himself down with and after a moment felt nicely in charge of himself.

"Good to see you after all these years, Celia." His eyes flickered over her; she had a feeling, as he continued his opening pleasantries, that she was being assessed, some kind of measure being taken.

". . . but you're a busy woman and I'm a busy man, I don't fool around. What's the story? About my letter, my fair share? I guess you agree it was a rotten lousy trick she pulled at the last minute—"

"But my husband wrote you—"

"Yeah, great letter, like shove it, brother." He came over and rested his big red hands on her board and leaned toward her and she felt a wave of physical fear, compounded with an instant natural dislike of him. Those stony dark eyebrows, that unforgiving jaw—

Ridiculous, people around, all she had to do was scream. Or walk out of the office.

He did, though, have a claim, she repeated to herself. No matter what Waldo said.

"It all has to go through probate, and the house has to be sold, and I'm told real estate is more or less at a standstill there as well as everywhere . . ."

Hearing herself temporizing, she thought, Waldo will kill me.

Here it was, the soft spot he was looking for. Bear in, bear down, forget Waldo for the moment, after all she was the heir, he wasn't. He felt and enjoyed her fear, her obvious inability to hurl a flat contemptuous *no* at him. As, in her place, he would have done. "Go whistle for it, baby, you haven't a prayer and you know it."

As when making a sale, he changed tactics. "It's good to renew family ties. All these years, eh? Can I borrow you from your office and buy you a drink?"

"No . . . Bernard." How odd to be calling a total stranger by his first name. "But thanks. I'm really very busy—"

"All right, I am too, as I said, and I know there'll be a wait, but Trenton's not all that far from New York, I'll be in touch, Celia, after all it's only right and proper, there are only the two of us left. Ta ta."

With an unconvincing grin, he bent farther forward and kissed her temple. He had a mouth which looked ruthless but felt warm and damp, oversoft. He turned and left and without thinking she took a tissue from the box at her elbow and brushed the place where his lips had been.

CHAPTER 5

I suppose, Celia said to herself, principles are all very fine until they get in your way, and then they become what other people as a rule should practice. In their absence all would be chaos. Principles being as much a matter of gluing civilization together as of personal ethics.

But not for you, right now, to practice. Because this, this that has happened to you, is somehow different.

But maybe all love affairs were like this?—Having moved without thinking, without planning, into a delicious dark, secret, and yet sunlit place.

She tried to scorch the sweet dark place with the harsh light of her own intelligence and active conscience.

She had, she agreed to herself, a perfectly all right marriage, reasonably happy, you didn't ask for the moon after twenty-five and anyway the astronauts trampling around had spoiled the moon and connected it up with the Pentagon.

Work that she loved, contentment at the end of the day, the nice apartment in Chelsea, the lazy scented hot bath making up for the morning's speedy shower, Waldo mixing martinis and pleasedly sniffing whatever it was she was cooking. Just enough partying, an occasional ballet or concert, plays, evenings out, Waldo saying, "Get out of your carpet slippers, darling, and into your Chanel Number Twenty-Two." Laughter shared—Waldo could be very funny about his day, about his clients and his artists—bed shared, peacefully and sometimes passionately.

It all clouded gently into ashes under her restless delicate probing fingertip.

A long striding shadow fell across the unreal buttercupped landscape. Cy's. Waking her to great pain and great joy.

Taking her away from her quiet meadow to soaring slopes and shining heaving seas and woods roaring with wind and promise.

"In the classic phrase," Cy said, "we can't go on like this."

They were sitting in a dark corner inconveniently uptown and on the West Side, well out of the way for both of them. A great many people knew Cy; Waldo's circle was wide and while hers was more limited interest among any of them would no doubt snap to attention at the sight of the silent absorbed couple, caught up very visibly in the light of their own private hearthfire.

"It's awful, isn't it," Celia muttered radiantly. "Like what?"

"Hiding. Skulking. No place to kiss you, really. Your hand is nice, and so are your eyes, but—"

Without discussing it, they had both rejected the idea of a shiny motel in Connecticut or Long Island, or an obscure hotel on some unfrequented street. The bland signing of the register, fake name, the brief hurried plunge into love. No peace, grace, music, touching of hands, no gathering quiet, laughter dropping away, no lightly savoring beforehand, no time for the delightful flickering butterflies in the ribcage. The careful and separate returns to be worried about, handled—"Where were you today, Celia, I tried to reach you at work and they said you hadn't come back after lunch—?"

"I wonder," she said to her glass of Cinzano, "if Waldo knows . . ."

He looked at her shimmer, her garden growing every day; in a way a creation of his. But no, that had always been there, inside her, she couldn't produce it if she didn't intrinsically have it, that summoned, waked beauty.

"Knows what?" he asked deliberately.

She gave him a brief stunned look and he said, "Go ahead, put it into words. I want to hear it, from you. I think you have a not unnatural tendency to look the other way. You're a peace-loving soul and a very nice woman, but there are times when you have to look straight ahead of you."

Which was exactly what she did, not meeting his eyes.

"Knows what, Celia?"

"That, for the time, at least . . ."

"Yes?"

"I'm in love with you," on a long sigh, but soft and clear.

"Well, then, look at me."

"I hardly dare to look at you in public."

"This is about as un-public as you can get, only those two men up there near the door half-sloshed—"

She had told him hesitantly, over the first sip of her drink, that she and Waldo were going away for two weeks or so. He was in a contained way furious, and was silent so long that he frightened her.

After a while, he said, "Whose idea was this, yours or Waldo's?"

"His. I didn't—don't want to. In a way, he threatened me . . . talked about renewing marriage vows . . ."

He looked even blacker. "A ladies' magazine journey, can this marriage be saved?—How on earth can he threaten you? What can he do if you decide to—"

He hesitated, and then said, "I'm getting as bad as you are, leaving things unsaid. But it's time to say them. What can he do if you decide to divorce him?"

It was the first time the ultimate, decisive word had been spoken between them.

"It's—it hasn't been," Celia said in an astonished way, "much more than a month . . ." Her eyes grave behind the solemn round shining glasses, contemplating the word month, and along with it the question of what time had or hadn't after all, to do with anything.

As though inside her head, he answered her. "It doesn't need more than an hour. Fortunately or unfortunately. When, finally, you know yourself and know somebody else. Most of us grow up late, in this country." And, thumb moving lightly across her palm, "Don't let anyone else conduct you across the street before the next time I see you."

He still had not told her about Waldo and Irena Tova. For a while, he had thought, maybe Waldo always has a girl on the side, maybe it doesn't mean all that much to him, maybe she knows and prefers peace and quiet and a settled marriage to a face-to-face housewrecking brawl; and maybe *she's* had compensating affairs, couples have their own private ways of finding their balance.

He had also though that perhaps what he was feeling could be dealt with and gotten over, get down to business, passion consummated, it's been nice, love, you go your way and I'll go mine, I don't fancy breaking up other people's marriages at the drop of a hat—

He knew now that in this he was quite wrong, permanently wrong; he had a ridiculous and raging feeling sometimes, waking in the night, that his own loved and cherished Celia, his own wife, might at that very moment be committing adultery with an impostor named Waldo St. Clair.

"As I said," not threatening, but gentle, hand hard and warm, tightening on hers, "we can't go on like this." He looked at his watch. "A lumberman will be waiting for me in ten minutes, he wants nothing less than the Monet, and if I can find him several more of the same brand he says he's in the market —which will you finish up, Celia, your Cinzano or your demitasse, or both? As things are, you're getting in the way of my business as well as my minute-to-minute concentration on anything, except you."

"What is it you want me to do—not go away with him?"

"Several weeks is neither here nor there, if he really wants to do some buying, and to hell with the marriage vows speech— no, I want you to make up your mind. I want to be committed to you and I want you to be committed to me. We've had our spell in the vacuum."

"And needless to say"—he slid off the bench of the booth,

stood up and held out his hand to her—"before you go, we will have our long overdue time with each other."

At close to two, by the bedside clock, she felt Waldo stirring, and, first delicate tasting, the back of one hand slipping across her breasts.

She had been awake but tried to make her voice sleepy. "Sorry, tonight, I'm *hors de combat*." A phrase inherited from her mother.

Waldo raised himself from his pillow. There was enough light from the illuminated dial of the clock to show his mouth and eyes, ironic.

"Funny, I thought that was all over two weeks ago, you said you were when we came home from that party—of course we'd both had a lot to drink—maybe my dates are wrong and maybe you forgot your dates too. Let's only hope, Celia, that you're not beginning to go through early menopause."

He withdrew thoughtfully to the far side of the bed, turned over on his other side, and went to sleep.

Celia was alone when the front doorbell rang piercingly. The door, not the downstairs buzzer—

She went and put her eye to the little glass hole that even the most confident and careless New Yorkers felt it a necessity to supply themselves with.

The man, magnified but seemingly falsely to be standing at a distance, was her cousin Bernard.

Oh, hell, she almost said aloud. But she hadn't been careful with her feet, walking to the door, and the old, fine parquet creaked resoundingly.

Waldo was at a gallery opening—"How you all do take in each other's washing," Celia said—or rather a loft spree with beer instead of champagne, in SoHo, south of Houston Street. She had no idea when he would be home. She had had her bath and fixed her own drink and had just begun on her book but found herself unable to concentrate. She was, mentally, deep in Cy's arms.

She opened the door with reluctance. He moved in fast and aggressively as if he thought he had been going to be denied entrance. Under the diamond shower of light from the little crystal chandelier, he made a fast and to her offensive study of her face, her body, in long apricot silk jersey slit to the knee on either side, touching her and not touching her, depending on how she moved.

"Gracious living, yet," he said. "Waldo here?"

"No."

"Good. Just the family. My, you have" moving ahead of her into the living room—"a nice place here," eyes raking the deep sofa, the mirrors, the pictures, the wall of books, the depths of blue in the Chinese scholar's rug. His eye finally lit on the filled glass on the brass coffee table where on an illuminated shelf six inches down lay Celia's collection of rare shells.

She had once thought shell collecting—barefoot, paddling, in Nantucket or Ocho Rios, Waldo soaking sun, half-dozing—interesting and absorbing.

"May I," testingly, "give you a drink? Or are you—"

"I've got all the time in the world," Bernard said heartily and discouragingly. "As I said, keep in touch, eh? In on business, and I thought, now we've met after all these years must look up old Celia." He flung his raincoat over a low white chair and settled himself solidly on the sofa.

"Scotch for me if you have it and don't spare the horses. It's cold as a sonofabitch out there."

As she poured his scotch, Celia thought, What a lovely family I have. Cy, it's too bad you couldn't have known my Great-aunt Laura but this is my cousin Bernard, my only other living relative . . .

He had met, or observed Bernard, though, crashing about at Hall and St. Clair, and asked her in a worried way what Waldo meant by his carrying a gun; and she said he ought to know by now that Waldo was a born dramatist.

Bernard emptied half his drink in one gulp and continued his survey of her.

"Great security system you have here. I was just looking for you name on the buzzer when a kid arrived delivering liquor and they buzzed *him* and I just followed him in. Of course, you don't have to answer your doorbell but you never know who it is, friend or foe, right? and you go and take a peek and that floor's a dead giveaway. Let's see—" He walked rapidly into the hall and said over his shoulder, "Lock's nothing particular, either."

Was he just joining the daily chorus about crime or was he trying to intimidate her in some way? Tell her how vulnerable she was, to silent footsteps on the carpeted stairs some night when she was for a while alone? The apartment was on the second floor of the brownstone, at the front, looking over a very quiet street.

He was gratified by the flicker of doubt, of a kind of remote fear, in the large dark eyes behind the glasses. Bet she's as blind as a bat without them, he thought. Helpless.

It was interesting to see that his cousin Celia, woman of the world, money, fancy apartment, wearing what he supposed were at-home clothes even if she was here all by herself, wasn't tough like a lot of New York women were. And that she frightened easily.

But what nonsense, Celia told herself. To feel exposed and invaded, threatened, just because an unattractive relative had landed himself on her on a night when she had been so happily alone and not alone. A bore. That was all it was.

He finished his drink and said, "While you're on your feet—" waving the glass at her. She made the second drink lighter but he looked as if he had a large capacity.

"Come sit down." He patted the sofa cushion beside him. "Time to talk. Don't look so big-eyed, I'm not going to ruin your evening, got a girl expecting me sooner or later, and your Waldo will be coming home to his pretty wife slit all the way up to the knees—" His leer suggested an immediate mutual toppling onto the sofa. "And you haven't even touched your drink."

She sat down somewhere between the cushion beside him and what would have been a forbidding huddle into the far end of the sofa.

"We were just getting warm the last time we talked. You saying probate would take a bit of time, so that we couldn't settle matters until that went through . . ."

"That isn't quite what I said."

"Well, I thought you'd be interested in something—you know how tatty the old bitch was the way she went about things, the dirty door, the canned milk, the mutt with salve and sores all over him. One day, last spring I suppose it would be, I brought along a bottle of cheap sherry, didn't dare drink a real drink in front of her but I thought she might join me. Especially if it was free, and did she ever, two whole big glasses, the first booze she'd probably had in a decade. You know those old ticking covers she's got over everything?"

"Yes," Celia said, wanting to push the dead room, the dead house, the dead aunt away from her forever; a stain on the warmth and joy that had been enfolding her before the doorbell rang.

"She hauled herself out of her chair after her second glass of sherry and pulled one of the covers off and showed me a chair, you'd think it was the throne of the Queen of England the way she talked about it, she said it was a Philadelphia chair, and all I thought was, so okay, this is Philadelphia, and it has a chair that lives here . . . d'you mind if I fix myself another small one? The last tasted like an ounce, and I'm not a man for single ounces—"

Coming back into the living room, he sat down uncomfortably close beside her, large, rumpled, red, but exuding a kind of abused latent power which was not at all reassuring.

With a sudden soft little brutal motion, he snatched off her glasses.

Just as he'd thought, the eyes with the confused melting softness of the extremely nearsighted; and in her case beautiful. This close, a kind of brandy color, was the way he put it, the light behind the bar gleaming through a precious and expensive bottle. Thick short heavy lashes like silk, and what he though of as Gore eyebrows.

"For God's sake—" Strangled fury in her voice, as she dove at his hand for her glasses.

He gave them back to her. "Just wanted to see your pretty eyes without the windowpanes. You look sort of like an aunt of mine, dead long ago, I suppose an aunt or cousin or something of yours—well, anyway, the chair."

"Finish your drink," she said icily. "I want my dinner and I want my evening and I'm not a furniture dealer, and it would be a little embarrassing to call the police to have them eject a distant member of the family."

"Just going. But this you'll like to hear. I saw in the *Times* this morning that the frame, mind you, just the frame of a Philadelphia chair that looked just like hers, claw-and-ball feet they call them, same arms, same back—but no upholstery, springs hanging out every which way—was up for sale at $95,000. Hers had a kind of yellowish seat, perfect condition, damask I guess—think of it, the chair could be worth more than the house—"

He dropped his voice conspiratorially, as if someone might be listening. And added, hungry nose to the bakery window,

"I mean, what if there was more of that stuff there, along with her tacky old odds and ends?"

He had been sorely tempted to hire a U-Haul truck and park it in front of the house and go in and investigate and help himself. Not, he conceded, that he'd know the good stuff from the bad but just grab it anyway, on the offchance.

He was in possession of a tempting front door key, acquired so long ago he had forgotten the circumstances. But there were deterrents. A cautious phone call to the house was answered by the aged black maid, Vera. Mr. Waldo St. Clair, she said, wanted her in residence until the house was sold. He knew she was protectively, passionately fond of Miss Celia, he'd had to listen to her on the subject all too often.

And he thought it likely that Prentice, who pulled weight in the city, might have requested a systematic police check on the house. It was a wealthy neighborhood and well patrolled.

A third shadowy reason was that in case he got caught, arrested, or threatened with it, for theft, the St. Clairs might have an ironclad reason for denying him what he now identified as his rightful fair share.

Think of it, the house and the chair alone if there weren't other things, jewelry, silver, that would bring in money, would entitle him to—let's deal in round numbers, he thought— maybe fifty thousand dollars. Enough to buy a business for himself. He knew of a nice little Ping-Pong ball factory in Paterson going begging; if he didn't pick it up soon, someone else would grab it. To sit back and tell other men what to do, and have them bring him wads of money, and with his experience he'd know how to deal with fiddled expense accounts and invoices—

His eyes sparkled at the lovely prospect.

So, just for the moment, don't rock the boat. He'd scared her, and the snatching off of her glasses had shown her a kind of ruthless naked fist, don't try anything with me, doll, I'm bigger and tougher than you are and I don't play by your drawing-room rules.

He drained his drink and got up. "You've got my address? Good. Not that we'll probably be writing to each other, now I've found your lair, hope to see you in a few days."

What was she to do with this incubus?

"We might as well get it straight right now," she said. "My husband is handling the house and everything to do with it. Not I."

"Screw Waldo," Bernard said. "I'm your blood, and you're my blood, right?"

He suddenly moved, hugged her unpleasantly hard, an embrace like a threat, gave her another damp kiss, this time on her cheek, and as she pulled hotly away released her, grinning.

"I'll let myself out, and you can at last get to your drink. Ta ta, Celia, my own blood."

CHAPTER 6

Waldo when he came home at eleven was in a controlled rage.

He had taken Irena Tova along to the SoHo opening and she had left after one glass of beer. "I have a cold coming on, Waldo, I'm off to aspirin and whiskey and bed and anyway this stuff is awful, and the racket—don't call me, I'll be asleep."

He had called her, four times, during the course of the noisy party—during which he found and bought a bicycle, padded, painted, and embroidered to look like a curling dragon, with a dragon's head growing from the handlebars, which he thought he might sell to a rich young madwoman in the East Sixties— and got nothing but the go-away-please sound of the ringing.

On impulse, unable to stop himself, he called Albert Bloomgarden's apartment. Employing his usual method when for any given reason invading privacies by telephone, he dredged up an unlikely name. "Sorry to bother you at this hour, is Etheldred there by any chance?"

"*Who?*" Bloomgarden asked. He sounded irritated, interruped at some important moment. "Etheldred? I'm afraid you've got the—"

There was a faint faraway ripple a distance from the phone. Irena's laugh, he'd know it in his coffin.

In every affair, he considered, what mattered vitally was who had the upper hand, who called the turn. Who had the better balance on the tightrope. Up until now, he had been dominant.

In the cab, he painted awful pictures for himself of what was happening or would be happening at Bloomgarden's apartment. A man of immense wealth, several times divorced, free now, although of course that wouldn't matter to either of them—

And her poor sweet Waldo, forever short of money, having to toe the line with his Celia, because she could tide them over when things were rough at the gallery. She might even have heard—they lived, in this business, in a violently gossiping incestuous world—that his wife was sliding into a love affair herself.

He had puzzled only a week about who this might be, of Celia's; and then Cy Hall had walked into a room at a party and, from a glow, from a crackling in the air, he knew, instantly.

Which might mean nothing, Cy was never without an attractive woman in his life; or might mean the whole goddamned ball game.

It was one thing to have Irena as a warm and separate and totally necessary part of his day, his week. It would be another to come to her as a rejected, cuckolded husband. "Celia says she wants a divorce . . ."

Leave it to me.

But what if, in the process of risking everything, you lost everything?

Hurry—

Little knowing she was walking into the lion's lair, Celia talked drowsily when Waldo brought a drink into the bedroom to take off his clothes with and read awhile with.

"You're very lucky you missed Bernard. He's been here, decimating the scotch."

"On your invitation?" Waldo was neat about his outer clothes, folded his trousers over a hanger, and then hung up his suit coat, stripped off his shirt, socks, and shorts and flung them in a heap on his side of the bed, and slipped in graceful and olive-naked beside her.

"No, he rang the doorbell and he heard me creaking while I went to see who it was, so I couldn't—"

Miles away, Walso said, "I suppose you'd let in a thief so as not to hurt his feelings if he heard you come to the door to see who it was."

At the hardness in his voice, and what might have been contempt, she said, "All right, subject of Bernard closed, I didn't want him, it would have been much nicer if you'd been home to conduct him to the door, he kissed me very damply and before that tore the glasses off my face—"

"You're fortunate in your relatives. Better you than me." Waldo, some kind of whiteness about his mouth, opened a biography of Augustus John.

"He was, in a way, slavering about that horrible house." Don't give in to the temptation to say to yourself, It's not Waldo here in our bed, it's Cy. Fasten down this wild balloon. Talk about family matters. As if they had some small importance.

"He went on and on about a Philadelphia chair she'd shown him, said it would bring a fortune—"

Waldo laid down his book. He stroked a thumb across the slight crease of bone between his eyebrows, a gesture that always meant he was thinking of something else and was not really there, with her.

After a moment, he said irritably, "I don't suppose he knows a footstool from a piece of flotsam—but I've asked you, once, twice, to go down there and see if there's anything you want—"

Half asleep, or wanting to be, Celia said, "Did you know that flotsam is what floats and jetsam is what sinks? I don't know where I picked that up—"

He lit a cigarette, smoked an inch of it impatiently, put it out and picking up his book said, "Thanks a lot for general information at midnight."

"Waldo . . . ?"

"What?" staring at his book but she thought he wasn't reading. "If you're feeling this way—sort of, Celia, will you please go to hell in a handbarrow—do you think it's wise for us to go off now together to have what you've described as a party?"

His back was to her, strong and finely muscled, as he put the book away on his own table.

"I have no idea what you're talking about, I'm dead tired as a matter of fact, but—" He rested his head on his pillow, eyes on hers. "Is there anything, anyone here *you* can't bear to leave behind?"

"No . . ." She wasn't ready for it, yet.

"Well, then—" Another of his lightning changes of mood, the seeking mouth, the warm arm across her body. "We're always a party, darling, aren't we? You come to mine and I'll come to yours."

She had felt so guilty after her cold and traitorous refusal of him the night before that she made herself respond.

Sliding off to sleep, Waldo murmured urgently into her hair, "Two days, thank Christ, only two days, and then . . ."

There was the sound of furiously fast typing from Cy's office. His door was closed.

The gallery was empty, morning-immaculate, smelling faintly of wax. Irena when she achieved her own mild eminence in their setup had not abandoned the plants; they had been freshly watered and sprayed, and they glistened dewily in the cold December sunlight coming in.

Waldo went straight to Irena's office, where she was sitting, shining with contentment, at her desk, dipping pieces of buttered croissant into her steaming café au lait which she always brought in from Gourmet Goodies two doors away.

She licked her fingers. "You caught me reverting to peasantry. Good morning, sweet." Then, lightly, eyes on his over the top of her Delft coffeecup, she said, "You look, funny word, dangerous."

"What the hell were you doing, at Bloomgarden's last night?"

"Oh, then, you were the Etheldred man, I thought so. I was eating caviar after that beer and potato chip muck downtown. And successfully resisting his advances. He's not"—as she consumed the last tip of the croissant—"my type. But the Marisol is s-o-l-d, and more than Cy was asking for it, and I won't let you spoil my rich happy morning."

The upper hand, subtly flicking defiance at him again.

Having made her point, she came over to him to be kissed good morning, her body melting vigorously against his.

"Tell me," dark blue eyes close under his, sparkling, the whites astonishingly fresh and clear after her caviar and no doubt champagne night, "does your wife really not know or suspect at all that you are wickedly involved with another woman?"

"No. She's up to here in her work, which she enjoys, and—"

"And you must then be always very loving, very devoted, to keep her so blissfully ignorant."

He felt as if a pair of giant shears was closing on him.

"I don't like to pry," Irena went on, murmuring almost to herself, "but naturally I think about it. More and more, lately. What is my own Waldo up to now, while he's away from me—"

Waldo was very pale under his olive coloring. Was this some kind of remote, tentative beginning to a breakaway?

—I love you but as we've agreed in the circumstances we can't marry. Of course for obvious financial reasons you must remain married but your attentions to your wife—to keep her from knowing about us, to ward off the horrid crisis of a divorce—are too much for me to contemplate, to bear, I can no longer live like this, imagining the two of you—

Was she thoughtfully balancing the Bloomgardens of the world, however much they were not her type, with her dear but strapped Waldo?

Was her own reaching thirty—it was her birthday, today— some kind of hell or high water milestone for her?

He kissed her hard and said, "Shut up, Irena, and happy birthday, which we will thoroughly celebrate."

She hadn't finished with it yet. "Thank you, Waldo. And then this journey abroad—did she suggest it, with the idea of— no matter what you say, and I can't imagine you married to a stupid woman—some reunion, reconciliation? A fresh start?"

The Waldo who at least outwardly met danger head on and coped with it took over. He calmly lit two cigarettes at once, gave her one, and said, "Mrs. Donahue is getting restive. She has a new drawing room, entrance hall, dining room, library, sitting room, and four bedrooms which require as soon as possible pictures by interesting Irish artists and if I don't supply them, to my own considerable profit, someone else will. And I don't have to go and eat caviar with her to cinch our agreement."

"Oh yes, the tugboat people—*Irish* painters?"

"You may be sure, Irena, that I will discover them in quantity."

The Tova money, not that it did Irena much good, came out of armaments in the Ruhr; but he saw that for the moment she was serene and purring again, hands very lightly stroking his hair.

"I'm looking forward to our celebration."

It was a busy morning. Christmas shoppers—mostly just shopping and not buying—strolled the white marble floors. But Waldo did sell one small Paul Klee and Irena disposed of a sculpture of large crystal hands folded about a stainless steel ball, priced at $1,850; she obligingly, after some dickering, knocked off the fifty. The sound of typing continued undiminished from Cy's office.

At eleven, he came out and went over to Waldo.

"Sorry to do this to you at this late date," he said, "but I can't make it after all and you've inherited the trip."

"What trip?" Waldo asked in instant and well-founded alarm.

There was to be an auction late that afternoon in Manchester, Vermont. "The collection rates Sotheby Parke Bernet but she's very old and insists that it be done at home, hell of a place to get to, dealers coming from California and every which way—Wahlgren is interested in the Veronese and I promised I'd see what we could do for him . . ."

"But Christ, Cy, I'm leaving myself, tomorrow night, and I have a million things to—"

"No way out, I'm afraid," Cy said kindly. "The last plane that'll get you there on time leaves at twelve-twenty from La Guardia, and I'm afraid you have to change at Poughkeepsie."

No way out, flamingly, right. If he was a partner, he was very much a junior partner, financially speaking; and Pierre Wahlgren was one of the gallery's best customers. Goodbye birthday party, and a warm and peaceful tying up of odds and ends with Irena, a restoring of the right footing with her. And almost in panic he remembered that he wouldn't be able to have her for lunch and love tomorrow. It was her weekly ballet class and she was always adamant about it.

She was standing just a few feet away; she must have heard him getting his marching orders.

"If you'll come along to the office I have a note somewhere of our top bid and his top price . . ."

No one could have told from Waldo's recovered alert and graceful demeanor that he was throwing several more logs onto his steady glowing fire.

"You're not eating properly," Cy said. "And your hand is cold."

They were sitting at a table by the window, overlooking a frozen-over pond, of a small inn near Brookfield Center, Connecticut. It had just started to snow, a thick soft gentle snow, not a whipping fall.

Making an attempt at her truffled pâté, Celia said—feeling a little drunk already although she had only had a glass of chablis —"Did you arrange this, too, the snow?"

"No, but it makes a nice anniversary."

Ten miles from where they were lunching, abstractedly and without appetite on either side, was Cy's brother Peter's house. "Nice and quiet, three fireplaces," Cy had said on the way up in the car.

"You sound like a rental agent . . ." Celia tried whisperingly for gaiety and felt at first only secrecy and guilt.

Peter and his wife and three children were in St. Agathe, in Canada, for a skiing week.

A chicken curry, small tart salad, crème caramel, demitasse; a jolt of eyes meeting.

Now at last—

Cy's fine capable hands almost uncertain as he paid the bill.

"Will it be all right, in the snow, the car, I mean? All these hills—?"

"I will undertake," Cy said, "To get you there and home again safely."

At four-thirty on the afternoon of December 17, Cecelia Margaret Gore St. Clair and Cyril Francis Hall committed adultery, with a great and consuming and decisive delight.

Celia, usually so good about packing, was going about it slowly.

Waldo looked at his watch. "You have half an hour more, and then one drink, and then the cab."

"Yes, all right . . ."

She looked at him with a kind attention; as at someone she knew well and once had been extremely fond of.

He knew that she wasn't, as he was, a creature of moods, of impulses; but, by nature, a constant sort of person.

He knew that he had lost her.

Just as well, all things considered.

CHAPTER 7

It was the usual semi-nightmare: the leave-taking, the journey.

Kind friends dropping at the last moment—

"I couldn't take myself home without stopping to say goodbye . . ."

"Waldo, a scotch for me if you will and if there's any lime juice handy Elouise likes a gimlet . . ."

"Celia, I brought along my black widow's shawl for you, divine actually, and Ireland is a devilish place for drafts . . ."

Waldo dashing about tending bar, refilling drinks, exhorting her not to forget their paperbacks, and would she check his closet to see if he had packed his doeskin jacket, he couldn't remember putting it in his bag and he wanted it badly.

The telephone—for you, Celia, for you, Waldo, for you, Celia.

Cy. "I know I'm breaking all the rules of polite behavior. Goodbye, Celia, goodbye my darling, for God's sake take care of yourself . . . Celia . . . goodbye." And in a different voice, "While I'm about it, if you'll put Waldo on I'll wish him bon voyage."

With a strange inevitability, Bernard turned up among the attractive milling chattering people, Bernard in the same raincoat, which when removed revealed an expensive battered checked tweed suit.

Waldo went over to him and said rudely, "We're just leaving, is there anything I can get for you in a hurry?"

"Anything brown—scotch, rye, blend," Bernard said, looking around him in a bewildered way. "Leaving for where?"

"Abroad."

"*Abroad.*" The high-colored features formed themselves into a scowl. "For how long?"

"Indefinitely," Waldo said. "I'm afraid you'll have to help yourself, in the kitchen—" as the doorbell rang again.

Bernard went directly over to Celia and interrupted a monologue from a thin woman who was telling her where to eat in Dublin.

"The chicken sandwiches at the Buttery in the Royal Hibernian are absolutely—and their own homemade lemon mayonnaise—"

"*Indefinitely?*" Bernard said, having to raise his voice. "Where to, indefinitely?"

Celia, trying to keep in touch with time, with reality, with order, method in departure, looked at him as if he had gone mad.

"Where? . . . Oh, Dublin first, as a base, we'll be roaming around, and then perhaps London, or Paris, or both, depending on—"

A snatched moment for a double check of the medicine cabinet. Yes, Waldo's sleeping pills had been packed.

"Where's Waldo, Elouise needs a refill—"

In the confusion, Celia forgot her absolutely essential raincoat, her showercap, her spare pair of glasses, and the loop of Russian sable it would have been so nice to bury her chin in, in the devilish drafts of Ireland.

Christmas was five days away; the Aer Lingus 707 was jammed with people going home for the holidays to visit relatives. There wasn't an empty seat. Waldo, who was capable of exercising thrift on occasion, had decided against first class although he thought the plane would be crowded; he and his wife had ample reason and plenty of time, oceans of it, to regret this.

He was by the window, Celia in the no-man's-land center, and on the aisle sat a man of about six feet four who had tremendous trouble trying to get his legs under the seat in front of him and kept shifting them, and groaning with confinement and discomfort and annoyance, for hours, before he finally went to sleep with his great sword of an elbow in Celia's lap. He snored.

The usual garnished dinner—"We'd better take six bites, or seven, we haven't eaten since . . . when?" Waldo said. "Then I'll get us some champagne for a nightcap and general indigestion cure, and to bubble all that booze away—God, did you remember to ring the aspirin? I don't think I'll risk a sleeping pill, morning will come though right now it seems unlikely."

The awkward business of having somehow to get over and past the Paul Bunyan legs next to her to get to the bathroom; the man in his rage at his seating space and at his dinner silently refused to get up. It was like climbing a stile in a meadow, but not as pleasant, and impossible to do with any grace.

And finally, intermittently, some kind of sleep.

He started on the interrupted rosary he had so often, in the past few weeks, recited to himself.

One Irish table, deep-carved apron, lion-mask centered, flowers and fruits and sheaves on either side, mahogany stained black to look like bog oak, c. 1780.

A carefully casual question, back in New York, "What did your old auntie's father do for a living?"

"He didn't do anything, as far as I know . . . raced his yacht, and wandered around Europe collecting things for his houses, he seemed to have a lot of them but I suppose they were all sold except for the place in Philadelphia, when he died . . ."

One Philadelphia chair, upholstered in gold damask, signed G. Bullevant, perfect condition.

Cy, looming. He had spoken to her on the phone before they left. Something like, "My darling, how soon are you going to tell him and get this all over with?" Cy as far as he knew was not a man of casual affairs, one-night or three-week stands. There was that attractive woman, Dorothy Amory, he often turned up at parties and dinners with, but she had a smiling independence of her own. Probably only affable bed companions when they felt like it.

One entirely unique lady's desk in pink and white marble with gold drawer pulls and miniatures on ivory set in an oval pattern in the slanting lid (he could swear the miniature in the center was Louis XIV.)

Distance had a way of making up your mind for you. What, back there, you valued. What, back there, you really wanted. A long brilliantly revealing telescopic view of you and your life.

Waldo, I'm so terribly, terribly sorry—and she would be, he could see her troubled face, hear her hesitant voice—but it's happened and it can't be undone. Cy and I want to be married.

A pair of bonheurs du jour by Martin Carlin. (A dead spit for another pair sold in the sixties, he couldn't remember the year, at Christie's, for somewhere around $250,000.)

The gallery. Perhaps in a play they could continue as partners; but not in life. Cy the conqueror, Waldo the reject. And that feeling of his, that Cy was thinking seriously of pulling out, devoting himself entirely to his books. Which was probably why he had so amiably added the name St. Clair on his sign, to assure some kind of continuity. Without his money to carry it, however, there would be no Hall and St. Clair, or not for long.

One American Queen Anne shell-carved walnut armchair.

Then what? Start all over as somebody's assistant, somebody's salesman, faceless, nameless, a new employee? If indeed there was a job to be found at all. "Forty, are you . . . ?" and "I'm afraid we can't begin to match the income you expect . . ."

One tulipwood marquetry triangular game table with bronze doré by Charles Cressent.

Well, I'm free now, Irena darling. Free for what? "Look, we're penniless orphans. Neither of us fancies canned tomato soup, and instant coffee, and darning . . . I was eating caviar after that beer and potato chip muck downtown . . ." and "I'm perfectly satisfied with the way we are, for the moment." Irena, glorying in the flesh and all the good things, major and minor, that went with its enjoyment, the expensive sensuously delightful things.

One Louis XV marquetry table by Oeben.

And afterward—his mind slipped lightly over the word—when he had a graspable future, he'd have all the time in the world. There need be no great splash and commotion of a headlining auction at Sotheby Parke Bernet. Piece by piece. He knew where the desire, and the money lay . . . All those covers. All those rooms.

One Philadelphia carved mahogany Chippendale highboy.

Cy, "No way out, I'm afraid." In another context, but not really. Of course his junior partner had been dispatched on an errand to Vermont so he could have Celia to himself. Her face, her manner had told him that. Over, finished. And Cy was not a man to hesitate when his eye lit on something he wanted.

Hurry—

Cy's arms around her, and his speaking warm long body, quiet now.

His voice, lazy. "We're almost . . . I think . . . indecently at home with each other already—I mean in the sense that we should be solemn and earnest about this tremendous moment," laughing against her throat, ". . . do you suppose we should get up and have a drink?"

"I'm so happy right here," muffled, head against his breast, "but . . . yes . . . perhaps . . ."

Wasps and bees. What were wasps and bees doing in the big guest bedroom with its fire lighted, throwing sweeps of rose and gold and shadow at the bed, over Cy's cheekbones and forehead and near crystal gray eyes. The bees were louder, swarming about her head, not frightening, but annoying, distracting, making it hard to hear his voice, soft, lips to her ear . . . or could it be an electric saw, the trees in the snow across the small frozen pond outside the restaurant window . . . ?

"Cy. I can't hear you."

"Wrong man," a pleasant cool voice said beside her.

The buzzing resolved itself into the sound of jet engines carrying them thirty-five thousand feet over the Atlantic. There was a sudden flopping motion in her ribs as the plane veered, lifted a little, and then sharply dropped.

"Turbulence, the pilot informed us," the pleasant voice went on. "Heavy headwinds. We will arrive approximately one hour later than scheduled time at Shannon Airport. I imagine the said turbulence woke you up. You seemed to be dreaming very happily, Celia."

CHAPTER 8

"Indefinitely," Bernard Caldwell reminded himself, swept out on a tide of guests. *Gone indefinitely.*

He could just see them in manor houses, whatever they were, and in villas and on yachts, Waldo St. Clair occasionally rousing himself to stand back and look and hem and haw at somebody's artwork. Out of his reach, the two of them, to hell with his claims and his needs and his right to share— He supposed you could spend months leisurely buying pictures.

Maybe selling his Great-cousin Laura's house from that mysterious region called Abroad, going to lie in some expensive sun on the profits—wine and music, peace and luxury, no sleet, no snow tires, no hustling for the next dollar.

He had been hotly following the real estate news in the Philadelphia papers. A house in Society Hill, $90,000; one on upper Delancey Street, $110,000. To say nothing of the possible riches within—that chair, perhaps more things like it, and he was sure the old bitch must have trays and trays of jewels somewhere, he'd spotted the gnarl of large rings under the white cotton gloves as she sipped her blasted tea . . .

Indefinitely. The word kept hitting him and he could feel the beginnings of another of his rages. He shoved the temptation away.

Have to keep a clear head about this. It could be the most important deal of his life, the turning point. You didn't make a sale by looking the other way, letting it cool, just when your prospect was ripe for the final, wrap-it-up maneuver.

He called the manager of the Ping-Pong factory in Paterson. Yes, it was still on the market. Fellow in New Brunswick inter-

ested, though. The manager was a friend of Bernard's, sympa-
thetic. And with Bernard on top, he knew he'd keep his job,
not new-broomed out.

"Look," Bernard said. "Can you do some fast double-talking
about a prior offer? Hold this guy off for a bit? There's some
money owed to me, real money." By now he believed this
implicitly.

"He's set up a meeting here for right after the first of the
year," his friend the manager said. "I'll do my best for you, Bernie, but if it's a firm offer and he's there with cash on the line—
and of course he might offer by phone before that—" Obviously wanting Bernard to make a clear and immediate financial commitment.

"Say you have to clear it with the prior offer no matter
what." Even talking like this, treating it as a matter almost
settled, soothed and reassured him. "Get in touch with me by
phone, collect, no matter where I am, I'll leave numbers and
addresses with you."

Euphoric, he thought of Waldo figuring he could snatch his
money, his future away—indefinitely.

Okay, buster, if you think you can flush me down it, it's not
that easy.

She's frightened of me, and as much as said I had a right to
my fair share. And *he's* very sure of himself. But nowhere near
my size.

All kinds of possibilities presented themselves. She might be
brought to fear, say, that something unpleasant and unspecified
could happen to her husband, unless they coughed up. The
police, he knew, tended in fear of their lives to back away from
family quarrels. Police anywhere.

Besides, there was the information he had, in a mental back
pocket, you never knew.

The job—it was after all a job to be tackled, a sale to be
made—couldn't very well be taken care of in Trenton, New
Jersey.

Brinner Brothers, Everything for Bowling, were obliging
about it. A few weeks off on his own time.

"My old Aunt Bridgie in Galway . . . she'll be seventy-five."

Business was slow at this time of the year, everybody crocked at Christmas parties.

He had just under a thousand in his savings account. He took it all out, telling himself it takes money to make money. He booked a seat on Aer Lingus two days after the St. Clairs left.

It's a small country, he told himself, it won't take me long to find them.

They had a tall stiff bloody mary at Shannon Airport, flew on to Dublin, took a Mercedes cab in the astonishing pitch dark to the Shelbourne Hotel on St. Stephen's Green, and in their usual first-day manner, after Celia had unpacked for both of them, fell promptly into bed to sleep.

Waldo had not economized on their accommodations. "We may have to do some entertaining and I don't fancy sitting on the beds."

They had, a little numbly on their arrival, approved the small rose-colored sitting room, the big bedroom overlooking the square, everything white and ivory, billows of chintz striped in yellow and patterned in rose and yellow tulips, a round table and comfortable tuliped chairs by the foot-deep sill of the tall windows hung in thin drifting white silk ninon.

Celia woke in her twin bed, marvelously rested, at four o'clock, blinked, told herself where she was, and listened to the showering sounds from the bathroom.

Waldo came into the room looking freshly minted, shaved, and immaculate, his skin rosy under the olive. She watched him, in his tulip-printed chair, pulling on his knee socks and then musing through his closet and taking out a pencil-striped dark gray flannel suit with a vest. White shirt with severe small black dots, currant-red wool tie. Watching him windsor-knot it, absorbed in his reflection in the pier glass on its white stand, she thought in a peculiarly objective fashion, he really is a very attractive man.

"Tonight, all play and no work," Waldo said. "If you'll ever

get yourself out of that bed, Mrs. St. Clair, I'll buy you a drink,
or several, and we will both wallow in Dublin Bay oysters, and
then maybe sole grilled on the bone. And Guinness."

Not only an attractive man, a sweet and companionable one,
most of the time, when a mood, a darkening of the spirit,
wasn't upon him.

But, as though there weren't two of everybody. There were
two of her.

One was perched on the stool at the Shelbourne bar beside
Waldo. Recording with pleasure the sapphire etched glass
panels rising from the broad-breasted mahogany bar, making in
effect a semi-private little booth of each pair of stools. The
tufted black leather banquettes against the dark shining walls
—real leather, it was nice getting used to things that weren't
fake, while traveling. The soft warm lights, the festive little
clink of Waldo's drink against hers, the first cold taste of an
authoritative martini.

The other was with Cy Hall, or running across a great lonely
expanse to catch up with him. Already he was frighteningly far
away, an idea, not a presence.

While she chatted amiably with her husband, this other continued the dialogue she had begun, fitfully, on the plane.

Clean break, clean start. Maybe unthinkable— But try. Try
hard.

". . . renew our marriage vows. It never hurts to freshen
them up . . ."

I take you . . . to have and to hold, from this day forward,
for better, for worse, for richer, for poorer, in sickness and in
health, until death (and not a love affair, but oh God, I think I
love him, could it be possible in this short time—?) do us part
. . .

She had been brought up a Catholic and remained one in
her own eclectic, on-and-off, free-wheeling way. Early training
had driven a conscience into her, tender, severe, often unanswerable.

Break up a marriage because you found someone while crossing a street that you wanted, needed more? Just reach out and grab?

Go jump, Waldo.

She knew he was attracted to other women—right now he was almost absent-mindedly studying a very young and beautiful auburn-haired girl across the bar from him, and being studied back—but she thought there was something about her he needed at the hidden center of his life. Ego, though, perhaps, on her part.

The wicked little counter-conscience said, With me he can go on doing what he loves, at the gallery, even when the pickings are slim there, we're financially okay even if not up to our knees in money.

No, not two of her, but three. The third one, detached, intelligent, self-knowing, standing off at a little distance so that the voice was almost too low to catch, You know very well something has started that won't and can't be stopped.

"Come back, Celia," Waldo said, very softly. Their eyes met, hers startled and guilty. He looked amused and a little rueful.

"All right, I'll ask you again. Another one, before we go off to the Gresham for our oysters?"

"Yes, please, Waldo."

He deliberately turned his side to the girl across the bar and touched his fresh glass to hers.

"Your health, darling."

"And to . . . our almost-fifth anniversary," Celia said.

CHAPTER 9

They were on their way, in the midnight darkness of six o'clock in the evening, to the house of an artist named Kelley Kelly, somewhere to the east of Malahide on the coast north of Dublin.

Waldo had said he was going to spend a leisurely day in what galleries he could find—"Go shopping or something, Celia, I know after your third gallery you're fed to the teeth"—and hired a small black Mercedes for them.

Not an addict of shopping, she had wandered the streets, studied thrushes and finches beside a pond in St. Stephen's Green, spent an absorbed half hour in a bookshop on Dawson Street, and bought, when it started to rain, a caped yellow raincoat that reminded her of the slickers of her childhood, with toggles to fasten it and a soft little black corduroy collar. It was a very pretty coat, and highly visible.

It was raining now, the soft straight-down Irish rain that felt as if it was coming without malice from a giant watering can held directly over your head.

Waldo was a fast but stylish driver. He knew the coast road well; he had, while in college, spent summers with a friend at the friend's aunt's house, a great stone Georgian manor near Howth.

They had turned to the east and were climbing a hill between woods when the engine made a peculiar sound. Waldo swore under his breath, topped the hill and began to descend it. The sound grew more pronounced. He drove the car onto the grass verge at the left, got out and lifted the hood. Celia watched his intent face in the light of the headlamps, herself unworried; Waldo was unexpectly good with cars, with any kind of machinery, his long delicate fingers adept at finding and fixing trouble. The rain poured down on his dark shining head.

He got into the car and tried to start it. A cough, and then silence.

"Christ, this would have to happen at the end of nowhere," he said. He tried three more times. Nothing.

There was no light in the darkness around them; there were no reassuring yellow squares of windows promising telephones, shelter, help.

"I'll have to hunt up a telephone booth or, don't laugh, there may be a garage around somewhere, new since my time here."

"Shall I come with you?" Celia asked.

"What, in those sandals?—and somebody might pinch the car. Keep your fingers crossed for me." Neither of them could remember passing a phone booth or a garage for the last five miles or so; he walked on ahead, fast, and in a few moments the lights lost him.

A car coming too fast over the crest of the hill all but side-swiped the Mercedes, which shook her out of her attempted patient composure. She was hungry and thirsty and bored, but had been telling herself that, while traveling, these things happened, you had to take them in stride.

Rain began to blow in the open window beside her and she closed it, increasing her sense of isolation. Now there were not even sounds to be heard, branches creaking in the soft wind, a remote whistling snort: a horse.

Breakfasting in their room, Waldo had favored her with bits and pieces out of the *Irish Times*.

"Very little crime in this country," he said, "but they save up what they have to offer in that line until *we* arrive," and read in his usual shorthand fashion, "Armed robbers . . . escaped from an English prison . . . bank clerk in Skerries shot to death . . ."

Skerries. Not far up the coast from Malahide. Silly to begin
to feel a far-off nervousness and an increasing aloneness. It was
just the beat of the rain on the roof and the hood, and being in
a strange country, and the feeling of, bathed in the dashboard
lights, appearing from without to unseen eyes like a decoy
duck.

There was a clanking and a near snort on the hillside behind
her. She recognized from pictures she had seen a tinker's caravan, but not one they'd put in brochures for tourists, stained
with dirt and rain, the horse impossibly old, how could the
poor thing pull such a weight; dim figures in a huddle visible
through the open back.

The caravan pulled up ahead of her and what was at first an
unfrightening figure approached the Mercedes: a tall strong
young woman with tousled wet red hair, a child of two or so
slung on her hip, carelessly exposed to the pouring rain. She
motioned at Celia to open her window. Thinking some kind of
emergency help was wanted—the child sick?—Celia rolled it
down. A strong grubby hand was thrust under the nose.

"Alms, for the grace of God," the woman said.

She was often scolded by Waldo for dropping offerings into
any outthrust palm. "Coffee, a cup of soup, hell, they'll just
head for the wine." She had often felt that this extreme concern for the proper sobriety of the ragged and down covered a
small personal meanness when resorted to by the scolders.

But the harsh aggressiveness of the woman put her off. Not a
request; a demand. She felt unwillingly in her raincoat pocket
and found only two coins. There was nothing between change
and the five-pound notes and travelers checks in her wallet.
Waldo had had his pocket picked last year and was now unwilling to carry money himself, but on the other hand liked to
have plenty of it available. "You be the banker, Celia."

"Shouldn't that child be covered up?" she asked, trying to
figure out how much or how little the silver represented; she
hadn't quite mastered the currency system.

"Ah, he's used to it." The dirty hand closed over the coins

and then opened as the woman studied, with an air of incredulity, the alms she had been given.

Her voice rose to a shriek. "Ye can't mean it! You with the fancy car and fancy coat, all nice and dry and warm, all brushed and fed and tidy, and the boy"—she rattled the two-year-old on her hip like a weapon—"cryin' for his bit of porridge—"

"I do mean it," Celia said with the fury of the kindhearted when roused.

The woman spat on the coins and threw them to the ground. She raised one arm high, and in a chanting voice as one pronouncing an unholy ritual cried, "The curse of God be upon you. The curse of God be upon your man. The curse of God be on your children and your children's children and all who you love." Adding in a practical everyday way, "And I hope you break your leg."

She bent abruptly to retrieve the thrownaway money and with a brief, horrible, over-the-shoulder grin, walked back to the caravan, in the rain. Before it started off, with more clanking and another despairing snort from the horse, a rough-haired young man appeared from the streaming woods with a gun cocked over his arm and a burlap bag, dripping something dark in the headlights, an animal's blood, in his hand. He jumped into the back of the caravan.

Just as it rumbled down the long hill, almost out of reach of the headlights, she saw him jump out again, with his gun.

To kill something else, Celia thought, and with another bag dripping blood rejoin his conveyance around some agreed-upon bend in the road.

Probably.

The feeling of being enclosed and trapped, bathed in light in the blowing darkness, a woman alone—you with the fancy car and the fancy coat—forced her to open the door and get out and move away from the car into the shielding spruces beside the road.

Before this instinctive escape, she had looked at her watch; it was a sort of game, up until then, not to look at it, just be patient, just wait, Waldo would be along momentarily—

He had been gone twenty minutes.

From not very far away, there was the terrifying crack of a shot, filling the night, coming from every direction. Had the tinker man, then, circled around her, had he shot at the car?

Without thinking, she turned and ran like an animal into the cover of the woods. "The curse of God be upon you—" Right now?

It was, she decided later, one of two stupid things she could have done. The other would have been to sit, illumined invitingly, in the car. She couldn't switch off the lights because she would be asking on bended knee for another near or direct-hit sideswipe.

No question of running, with the uneven sloping ground, thickly treed. It could be a little hill of forty feet or so or an enormous plunge into a distant valley, there was no way of telling. More a matter of fingering your way blindly from tree to tree, each bole feeling like a mothering fortress; if you were flattened against it the less chance there was for the now silent gun to find you.

If, at all, it wanted you. This was Ireland, safe sweet Ireland. The peaceful republic, not the violent bloody north.

And the tinkers shot and killed animals, birds, for the only acceptable reason: to fill empty stomachs.

I'm a live rabbit frightened by a dead rabbit, Celia told herself, trying to tease away the primitive fear of the hunted, the doomed.

Somewhere, blessedly, "*Celia!*" Waldo's voice.

From behind her? Or to the right? The wind, rising now, distorted the cry.

"*Waldo . . .*" more a released scream too long held in than a locating answer.

Another shot, close. Dear God, Waldo mistaken for a rabbit or taken for his money; or thought to be somebody's estate agent after poachers and being warned away?

Close your throat, don't scream, don't send out an invitation to the man with the gun.

She had no idea whether she had been making her way through the trees parallel to the road, where Waldo should be, or at right angles away from it. She didn't dare call his name again but started, in what seemed to be a clear space, from the sound of the rain—no stir and loom of branches overhead, no protection from the blanketing pour, only sighing high grass— to run uphill.

Uphill must be right, to get back to light, safety, Waldo. Until now, she'd been going down.

There was someone behind her, close, running. She wanted to cry Waldo's name again but her throat wouldn't let her. Trees or no trees, she flung herself forward.

The burlap bag dripping darkness, the small extinguished life, for the hungry pot . . .

This must be what the rabbit felt before extinction, a blindness, a blankness. But no, they froze, became part of the landscape. Or were they just erect, resigned, saying, All right, death.

There was a sudden tremendous flare in her eyes which she thought, fleetingly, was some kind of giving-in of the brain.

A soft voice, male, said, "I don't suppose by any unlikely chance you've seen a three-legged beagle, ma'am?" And then seeing her frantic face, "Ah, sorry, you're in trouble, and who is it that—"

The light from his huge flash went yards behind her to find Waldo, sprawled full-length over a bony protruding tree root, gasping and wiping water out of his eyes with the back of his hand.

"Oh God, oh Jesus, Celia—" He ran to her and held her. She had never felt Waldo shaking all over before, and in a way it forced hysteria away from her. She put comforting arms around him.

"I thought you might have been shot—I didn't know where

you were calling from—I was trying to run to you, not away
from you—Waldo, it's all right—"

She hoped that the kind rescuing man with his light thrown
upon darkness would find his three-legged beagle.

Waldo raised the hood again, hands still shaking, took a
small metal object from a Pliofilm envelope and bent to the engine, raising his voice over the rain to Celia, talking faster than
he usually did.

"He couldn't come along himself, busy with his wife and the
midwife, the thirteenth child and he looked as if I was to con-
gratulate him! Thank God he had the part, anyway . . . what
on earth made you leave the car with all these guns around?"

As they started off, smoothly now, she tried to explain without a great deal of success fears that sounded frail, unreal, the
sense of being vulnerable to some unknown thing in the
lighted car in the night, and the acrid aftertaste of being cursed
down the generations by a redheaded woman from a tinker's
caravan.

"She didn't leave you out, Waldo, you're included."

He seemed far away, only half-listening. He looked drawn
and pale.

She felt a surge of guilt at frightening him the way she had,
running from him, thinking he was doom at her heels.

"That was thoughtful of her," he said, and lapsed into silence for the rest of their journey.

Kelley Kelly was a gentle mild man. His wife had the face
and air of a hellion. They lived in a small stone house on a hill,
also inhabited by three Airedales, four cats, and a cageful of
finches. The room smoked from a badly drawing fire of damp
peat; the clutter and dust were remarkable.

Celia knew immediately that dinner when provided would
be frightful.

A considerable amount of gin was consumed before the eye-
stinging fire, and then they went out to the stone studio behind
the house. Kelley Kelly's present phase was huge semi-abstract
canvases of blurred birds, in rain and cloud and haze, a confu-

sion of wings and motion, a sort of music flying at you. Waldo bought two of them; prices were discussed inaudibly in a far corner of the studio.

The telephone rang while they were having one last drink before dinner. Mrs. Kelly was rudely examining Celia, head to toe, as her husband handed the phone to Waldo. No privacy was possible; the instrument was on a table beside the fireplace.

"Irena." Neutral low voice. "Yes . . ."

"Let's talk a bit so he can transact his business in peace— Look at her, Kelley," waving a derisive hand at Celia. "Look, the way she can't take her eyes off the man, she's in love. How *nice* to be all flushed up in love with your husband after—how many years?"

"Five." She just saved herself from putting her hands to her hot face. Of course, Cy wouldn't be coming on, from New York, and under no circumstances could he ask for her.

"Yes, it is nice," Kelley Kelly said. "After all, we can't all take top honors as the parish bitch." He said this to his wife with a fond smile. She continued to stare at Celia, over Waldo's yeses and noes and that's-goods . . . "Tell Mrs. Donahue I'm hot on the trail and I've already bought three pictures for her." And his soft cool, "Well, then, goodbye, Irena Katrina," which was understood by the two of them as, Darling, I love you and I miss you and I'm half-dead without you.

"My God, the potatoes," Mrs. Kelly shrieked. "Am I the only one who smells something burning?"

At a table occupied in addition by two squatting cats, they ate the potatoes, which their hostess unsuccessfully tried to descorch with vinegar, greasy fried smelts, and canned spinach under a heavy fall of nutmeg. Waldo entertained them with his tale of the lost three-legged beagle and the tinker woman's curse.

"Undeserved, I hope," Mrs. Kelly said to Celia with her mouth full of smelts. "The point is not to believe in it. If you *do* believe in it, it works, and many's the time I've seen it work, people just withering and wasting."

She added with ghoulish glee, "If it had been me, now, in the woods, dark and all, guns around and Kelley here hard behind me, I think he might have seized the golden opportunity of doing away with me, who'd know who was responsible? And then he could spend the rest of his days with the egg girl, admit it, Kelly, you have an eye for the egg girl."

"For Jesus' sake, woman, he'll want his money back," Kelly said. "Everybody sit still while I get us some brandy and we'll drink curses and murderers away."

When they got back to the Shelbourne, there was a telegram for Celia at the desk. She didn't want to open it in front of Waldo, but there was no choice.

"Now you're the one with the shakes," he said. "Here, give it to me," and took the envelope away from her.

It had been sent from New York. It said: "Following you. Bernard."

No dates, no times, no places. Waldo sighed. "Persistent bastard. It's a good thing I married you for your income and not for your family connections."

"If he's going to make it his life's work to hector us," Celia said, "I thought we'd hand the house over to him—let him take care of selling it, after all that's what he does for a living, selling. If he got a decent price we could give him a cut—you can figure out how many thousands would keep him quiet. I won't have him forever at our heels."

This suggestion, which she considered both practical and fair, startled him into sharp anger.

"Celia—are you crazy? That half-assed crook, I wouldn't trust him to sell me a used tricycle."

In a manner not usual with her, but bruised and tired by her evening, her night, her dinner, and her longing thrust back and pushed away, she said in a small hard voice, "It's my house, Waldo."

He changed tactics. "We're both tired, let's drop it for the moment and drop into a bedtime scotch in the bar. Following you, indeed. What d'you suppose he means? In his thoughts? In his prayers? Or in his too solid flesh?"

He had got himself back again and was absurdly pleased with his speculations about Bernard. The simple message, participle and pronoun, had felt a little different to Celia: in an understated way threatening.

CHAPTER 10

Bernard got his own share of heavy headwinds and turbulence, crossing the Atlantic. He studied his planemates with haughty aversion and said to himself, bunch of parlormaids and cooks going home to see old Mither. A very fat woman beside him unwrapped three hot pastrami sandwiches which breathed at him as she consumed them. Wrong nationality, those sandwiches. He thought it and then said it aloud and was rewarded by a pale blue glare and a bridling of massive shoulders.

At Shannon Airport, he hoisted himself onto a bar stool without the grace of the St. Clairs and ordered their morning arrival drink, a bloody mary, from the same bartender.

"You can keep the Atlantic Ocean," he said to the bartender after his first gulp.

"Thank you. A nice bit of real estate. And while you're at it, does that include offshore oil rights?"

In his lonely way, Bernard fell into a conversation with him. Yes, he was visiting relatives here, rich relatives. As a matter of fact, just between us, there are expectations . . .

He had been drinking whiskey all night. His head felt like a balloon.

After his bloody mary, he wandered about the duty-free shopping area; and, as salesmen do, responded to the persuasions of other pitchmen. He bought himself a Black Watch tartan tie, a sterling silver shamrock tiepin, and an indestructible-looking brown tweed hat. For Celia, he bought as what he called a sweetener a bottle of Lanvin's Arpège toilet water.

After the short plane trip to Dublin Airport, he checked in at his small shabby hotel off O'Connell Street. He was tempted to go out and find a comfortable body but resisted it. This was a foreign country, you might catch something. And in any case you want to get a good solid rest, fella, from now on you need your wits about you. Because it's now or never.

It took Celia a while, on that late morning of wet crisp air and thin sun, to figure out why Dublin at Christmastime reminded her of Dickens.

There was a mysterious and all-pervading deep acrid odor, and a haze, part moisture and part diffused smoke, which made the ruddy brick buildings on the street she walked look like old lithographs of themselves. It was only from reading and not from any personal experience that she identified the smell and the blur in the air: soft coal burning, cheap, long since banished from more affluent cities.

But it did put you squarely back in the past in a way that was not unpleasant.

As always when strolling, she had her notebook with her, and paused to sketch the pattern of a railing here, a cornice there, the dappled design of rusticated stonework. From O'Connell Street, she made her way up busy Grafton Street, with its shops and swarms of Christmas shoppers, to the bare-boughed quiet of St. Stephen's Green. There, with expensive hotels nearby, the Royal Hibernian, the Shelbourne, the Russell, the soft-coal smell seemed to vanish.

She was sitting sideways on a bench trying in her notebook to record the pewter-silver bole of a beech tree—or no, it looked more like the pelt of a glistening wet seal—when a long shadow, and a footfall, made her look back over her shoulder.

She felt a tingle of shock in her fingertips.

Bernard, hands in his raincoat pocket, came to stand over her.

"You really meant that telegram literally, didn't you, following us," she said angrily.

He sat down beside her and put an arm across the back of the bench, behind her shoulders.

"I was a long way behind you when I spotted you on O'Con-

nell Street. I've just gotten out of bed, couldn't sleep on that
bloody crammed plane, and my legs aren't up to speed yet.
Anyway, I saw you stopping to draw things, and I didn't want
to interrupt while the iron was hot—but greetings, Celia, I
told you we'd keep in touch."

His approach was apparently unchanged: a false, grinning
assumption of family ties backed up by a promise of nose-to-
the-grindstone persistence. And by an unspecified physical
threat, the secret following, the arm almost touching her shoulders, the big ill-treated yet still powerful body too close, indecently too close.

Reaching for her handbag on the ground to put her sketch-
book away, she managed to move a few inches from the heavy
warm thigh.

"I had time due me," he explained, "and I thought, what the
hell, I've never been out of the U.S.A. unless you count Korea,
why not see what old Celia and Waldo are up to, get together.
Maybe look up my mother's cousin in Galway although I
doubt she's worth a penny, probably chickens in the parlor and
a pig in the bedroom. What d'you say we three gather round
for dinner, I brought along some letters and things you and
Waldo might be interested in, to get back to the matter of the
old bitch's leavings—"

"I wish to God the place would burn to the ground," Celia
said childishly, and then regretted having been so recklessly
open, so easily victimized.

He looked startled. "What, for the insurance? We could
think about it, but I don't think it would bring a lot, and we
might be caught with the kerosene cans . . ." He winked at her.
The undisguised villainy, in someone else who had nothing to
do with her, might have been amusing.

"About dinner," recovering herself, "will you telephone the
Shelbourne at say five o'clock? Waldo's lined up a number of
artists and we may be spoken for."

Enraging not to be able to say, Go away, get lost, I don't
want to have dinner or anything else to do with you ever,
you're a total stranger and I don't like you. At all. Or, more

directly, to borrow (censored) from Waldo, go screw yourself, Bernard.

Still not entirely sober, Bernard said, "I was going to suggest a drink, noon's staring us in the face, but you look like you're on the wing. To get Waldo's appetite for dinner up, you might say to him, call it a kind of code—Adela's on Seventy-sixth Street, and then around the corner a yellow awning, or canopy, rather—anyway, lousy place, Adela's, for my money, nothing but omelets, I stopped in one day after I—"

He seemed, abruptly, to hear what he was saying and looked chagrined. "Cards to the chest, Bernard," he solemnly informed himself. "Forget it, Celia."

With an air of purpose, people to be met on time, pressing things to be seen to, she got up and left him with a brief cool goodbye.

On her way to the corner of the Green nearest Dawson Street, she examined the cards he clutched to his chest. Not very hard to read, if he wasn't making it up. Waldo, omelet lunch with somebody, and then around the corner, a yellow canopy, an apartment house—people didn't go to two restaurants at midday.

From the accompanying leer, and "call it a kind of code" she filled in a woman, and from his point of view a leisurely afternoon bedding down. Perhaps on the other hand an ordinary client lunch, Waldo was a entertaining professional luncher. A demitasse and brandy at someone's apartment—"Do you think this would be a good place to hang the Matisse?"

Without her working at it, Irena sprang into her mind. Attractive, very, in a basic glistening healthy way. Waldo's daily workmate. Celia herself worked with pleasant personable men and knew the pull of mutual interests, shared coffee, company laughter and gossip.

Before she could stop herself, she thought in perfect naked honesty, How wonderful that would be, for Waldo and me. How absolutely wonderful.

At close to five o'clock, she was having her bath and Waldo was studying a painting he had bought in a gallery on Dame

Street. He didn't like it much but he thought Mrs. Donahue would love it. A ruined stone manor house clasped in ivy, under brooding poplars, with a woman in white, dimly seen, infinitely lonely, looking in at a yawning dark window. It was blurrily, beautifully painted; he needn't after all apologize to himself for it.

There was a loud unrefined knocking at the door.

He got up to open it to Bernard and the two men exchanged stares. Waldo had been trying on a heavy linen hacking coat in oatmeal color which Celia had bought him, as a present, on approval. He wore this with pale blue boxer shorts—he hadn't gotten around to his trousers—and black knee socks.

"Well, deshabille," Bernard said, making an unsuccessful stab at the pronunciation. "Did Celia tell you about getting together for dinner?" He moved aggressively into the room, five inches taller than Waldo and a third again his size. "I thought I'd come around instead of phoning, seemed friendlier—and then I thought if you did happen to be tied up we could at least have a sociable drink together, up here."

His gaze went around the rose-colored sitting room with its ruby and orange cannel-coal fire in the grate, and through the door to the creamy flowered big bedroom beyond.

"I'd say you know how to make yourself comfortable. Expense no object, of course." A gust of whiskey hit his unwilling host. "You ought to see the crummy dump I'm in. Off O'Connell Street. Whores and beggars taking shelter in the side doorways. And the radiator knocks."

"Too bad you didn't have yourself announced," Waldo said. "You would have been told we are not at home. Which we aren't, to you." He walked to the door and stood with his hand on the knob.

Celia, hearing their voices, came into the sitting room in a white robe. "I told you to call first, Bernard," she said mildly—there was something that made her feel vaguely guilty about his tired uncared-for look in this warm charming room—"and we are going out, as I'd expected."

"Well, let's have a drink anyway before you go, I'll order up a bottle if you haven't a drop of something around. As a matter of fact"—he felt in his breast pocket, under his raincoat—"I have something to show you you might be interested in."

Waldo lightly put his manners back on. "I very much doubt we would, but take off your coat and sit down, we have twenty minutes or so." He went to a walnut cabinet and took out glasses and a bottle of scotch, lifted the telephone and ordered ice.

With his customary boldness, as he made the drinks, he asked, "And what brings you to Ireland, Bernard, besides family ties?"

"Business brings me. What makes the world go round brings me," Bernard said. "Money."

"And what are you selling or trying to sell now in the line of business? Besides mysterious documents in your pocket."

"I'm at the moment in bowling alleys," Bernard said defiantly. "And collateral equipment. But I've got my eye on a little venture for myself, a Ping-Pong ball factory, and I intend to get some cash together and buy it."

"I think you've come to the wrong place, I thought they left *here* to go and find the streets paved with gold."

"I think I've come to the right place," Bernard said, and raised his glass. "Cheers."

He had sat down gingerly on a French open-arm chair upholstered in rose and ivory silk. His saluting glass had the air not of a festive gesture but a fist shaken in the face.

"Now then," Waldo said. "What's that in your pocket, to while away the cocktail hour?"

Reaching, Bernard said fumblingly, "It's only one of a lot of things that I— However, a step at a time. No point in going to court and letting the legal eagles get at it, they'd eat the house up between them—much better a peaceful settlement among us. There's this letter, from Great-cousin Laura. Do I have the floor?"

He unfolded an old thumbed sheet of paper, lips working, reading to himself, then cleared his throat and read, "I think of you, Bernard, as my only stay and support and *so* look forward to your visits. To Celia I'm obviously a burden she picks up once or twice a year—although I'm only a train ride away—and as there are only the two of you naturally I spend a great deal of time comparing the attentions offered a lonely sick old woman who happens to have even at her age an excellent memory—"

"I don't believe it," Waldo said amiably, lazily. "Not that it means a damned thing, the woman's wanderings, but I suspect you're making it up as you go along."

Savagely, Bernard thrust the soiled paper at him. Waldo gave it a careless glance, crumpled it in his fist, and tossed it accurately into the heart of the fire. There was a pale yellow flame dancing above the deep ruby glow, and then a whisper of gray ash.

"Just as I thought," Waldo said. "Fabrications, to put it politely."

Celia had never before seen a man's jaw literally drop.

Pouring obscenities, Bernard shot to his feet, reached into his suit coat pocket for something, and threw it. It just missed Waldo's head and crashed against the wall, and a flood of the fragrance of rock-garden flowers drenched the air: Arpège.

She heard herself cry out, saw Bernard, towering over Waldo, snatch him to his feet, fist raised; and then another cry, Bernard's, as Waldo raised a ruthless and accurate knee. Bernard bent double and stumbled back and then inarticulate with rage and pain made as if to fall again on Waldo when there was a light knock on the door.

It opened and an elderly maid said, "Sorry to disturb you, will I just turn back the beds for you—" and examined the scene, the great panting man, the nice-looking one in his underwear, the broken glass along the wall, the young woman clutching her white robe, and the smell, dear God, sickening really. They can say what they like about the Irish, she thought, but these Americans drink too much.

Outwardly unruffled, she went on into the bedroom and could be seen folding the spreads and turning back the white linen sheets with composed hands.

"All right, your round," Bernard said thickly. He reached for his raincoat and pulled it on. "And with Celia here—we men can get together privately, some other place, a bit later, there are things not quite fit for a lady's, a wife's ears—even though, these days—"

"Get the bloody hell out of here and stay out, next time I'll have the police on you," Waldo said. Celia thought it might perhaps be too bad for Bernard that he didn't know Waldo better, and necessarily couldn't read the white patches under the olive, in the center of his brow and on either side of his nostrils.

After Bernard's door-slamming exit, waves of violence overlaid with overpowering sweetness still filled the room. The maid, in the doorway, said, "I'll just get a brush and pan and clean up your nice bottle of broken scent."

After she had gone, Celia said, "Why did you burn his letter, Waldo? Candy from a baby—"

He turned sharply at the musing sound of her always soft voice.

"That, and your knee." She looked distressed.

"To your first question, I wanted to show him whom he's dealing with. You seem singularly unable to dispose of him and life is too short to put up with the Bernards of the world."

"But there was nothing to be afraid of, I've gotten the same kind of letter about him, from her, and if there was any direct promise of property you can be sure that would be the first thing he'd read to us."

"And your second," Waldo said calmly, "that bottle was a terribly near miss. And as for his fists, he's bigger than I am and I didn't fancy being thrown onto the coals on top of his letter. In his blundering way, he's a dangerous man. Do go put your clothes on, I'm starving for oysters."

While they waited for the elevator, he said, "What's all this, not for a lady's ears? Has he been talking to you, about me?"

"No, just that I might mention to you a restaurant named Adela's and a yellow canopy around the corner—to get you to join him for dinner." Her eyes on his were interested.

The white under-the-skin pattern appeared, but only in a brief flicker this time.

The elevator stopped for them.

On the way out, he went to the desk in the lobby. There were three or four people within earshot, not counting the pages whom Celia found enchanting—small thrush-voiced boys of eight or nine in dark green suits and shining mopheaded blond and dark haircuts, half upright and half sleepily sprawled on a bench beside the revolving doors.

The fair slender girl behind the high desk was already a devotee of Waldo's.

Not troubling to keep his voice down, Waldo said, "We've just been subjected to a great nuisance, in our rooms. Will you take note, and pass it on to your confreres? If a man comes into this lobby, wearing a tired-looking raincoat, and with a broken nose that could have been reset better—looks like a failed prizefighter, or a salesman up to his ankles in whiskey—will you kindly the next time, for our physical safety, immediately notify the police after you've warned us? And hold him here, and say we're out but expected any minute?"

In an amused bewildered way, the girl behind the desk said, "Yes indeed, Mr. St. Clair—if we spot him, that is—and has he a name to go with the rest of him?"

"Caldwell," Waldo said. "Bernard Caldwell. A remote family connection—you know how it is—but I'm afraid, a bit dangerous.

CHAPTER 11

You didn't realize the degree to which you were under the control of weather, of light, until the taken-for-granted was sharply altered.

It was eight-thirty. They were having breakfast and it was depthlessly dark outside, night not yet waked up.

Celia caught a sudden eavesdropping reflection of themselves in the black panes. Round table by the window, with a pink linen cloth to the floor. Glisten of silver, of crystal. Waldo, up ten minutes before she woke, had ordered tomato juice and coffee, ham and eggs and toast. He liked an ample breakfast when he was traveling. The kitchen had tactfully supplied, along with the tomato juice, Worcestershire sauce, fresh lemon wedges, and a slim bottle of Tabasco, in case they might want their breakfast fueled with gin or vodka.

She kept her studying gaze on the reflection as she ate a piece of toast. Waldo with his dark hair half in his eyes, cane-patterned brown and white robe, long hands busy with his ham and eggs. She in her white robe, light catching her glasses, erasing her eyes. In a momentary slipping of identity, she thought, Who are we? Two strangers, lost, nowhere, deep in some unlikely night.

She thrust aside the sinking sensation, the faint panic. All this nonsense because the sun rose, in Ireland, at a later hour than she was accustomed to at this time of year. All the same, she found she had suddenly decided to call Cy, in a way to remind herself who she was. If, that is, she kept her nerve and didn't change her mind.

Perhaps he had changed his. Distance, time for rational

thought, the warm steady blaze turning out to be merely the infatuation of a few weeks, a month. She thought that in spite of his work, his gallery, his books, his friends and clients and no doubt attractive women and eager hostesses, there was a certain loneliness about him. Which had caused him to reach out a hand to a young woman in glasses who was rejoicing in the snow and thinking about getting out her sled.

Her throat ached with tears. Yes, *lost* . . .

Not liking what was happening to the mouth of the woman looking back at her from the panes, she devoted herself to pouring each of them more coffee.

Waldo didn't look lost but as usual absorbed in the moment, gracefully switched over to left-hand-fork eating. "Incredible, the eggs," he said. "They must have been laid right outside the door ten minutes ago . . . what's the matter, Celia, did someone step heavily on your grave just now?"

"It's just the dark, it gets to me . . ."

"I like it," Waldo said. "Change, drama. Speaking of graves . . ." An appreciative bite, chewed, swallowed. "This soda bread makes the best toast I've ever tasted . . . do you remember where we put our wills?"

Startled, she gave her three-cornered smile that lit her quiet face. An abrupt change of subject, but in a way a help.

"Why? I mean, just at this moment, over your new-laid eggs . . . ?"

"I dreamed our plane crashed going back, or going somewhere, and you swam to shore—and the less said about that the better, probably the Dublin Bay prawns. I thought at the time they had a heavy hand with the sherry."

On their marriage, Celia had insisted that they draw up brief wills to each other. A sister of her father's had died intestate and a large estate had been chewed up in the courts before her heirs got their hands on the much reduced remainder; the losing battle over Aunt Cecelia's money had become a Gore family legend.

Guilt twanged at her. Waldo asleep beside her, dreaming, drowning, dying. She swimming to shore, safe.

"They're in the bottom right-hand drawer of the lacquer desk. Tucked into," she added accurately, "your grandmother's hymnbook."

It was one o'clock here; it would be eight o'clock in New York.

Celia, with a heavy pocketful of handsome Irish coins, walked through the rain on her way to meet Waldo for lunch at the Buttery in the Royal Hibernian, and stopped and went into a public telephone booth at the corner of St. Stephen's Green.

She felt shamed, furtive, uncertain, and thought the call probably ill-judged, after all; it would come to nothing. People did not respond with articulate passion over their morning coffee.

It came to nothing.

An answering-service girl said, "Mr. Hall is in Paris until the Wednesday after Christmas, is there any message?"

No, no message.

Paris somehow seemed farther away than New York. She had no way of placing him, seeing him there, as she saw him in his office with the easel in the corner and the smoke blue and amber rug on the floor, the sound of his typewriter, a ray of sun glowing through the Waterford crystal decanter on the drinks cart by the window.

Was he doing research for his book? Or merely shedding New York's Santa Clauses and omnipresent canned hymns and crowding, fighting shoppers for another city, another flavor? Her anxious mind supplied some ravishing woman. "I always spend Christmas with Amelie . . . we always go to midnight mass at Notre Dame together . . ."

She gave Amelie a house on the Île St. Louis, or at least a very beautiful apartment looking out over the Seine. She had forgotten her boots in the worry about calling New York and her suede gillies were drenched and squelching. A wind, malicious for gentle Dublin, hit her hard from the east and tried to whirl her umbrella out of her hand.

Cy Hall. Who was Cy Hall? And who was the woman held in his arms when he stopped the car on the way back from Connecticut, hearing him say, above her head, over the sound of his heart against her cheek, "I can't let you go, how can I let you go . . . ?"

The Buttery was all cheerful commotion and tartan upholstery, with elegantly dressed youngish men, bearing no remote resemblance to the American vision of red-headed freckled Irish, crowded around the bar three deep, talking advertising, publishing, politics.

Waldo, naturally enough, had one of the best places, in a corner, and had her martini waiting for her.

"Here's my wet hen, although you look—"

She had drawn glances when she came in, her hair blown about, her color high from the cold and wet, something about her, a coming-and-going radiance and moodiness. As always, she was remarkably but easily well-dressed, today in a trouser suit of powdery pale brown Donegal tweed, a whirl of Hermès scarf, sapphire and ruby and cream, about her throat and one shoulder, a soaked but dashing ruddy brown suede cape.

Finding Waldo's questioning, penetrating glance disturbing, she recalled the impromptu farewell party before they left.

"We're under strict orders from Melanie to eat chicken sandwiches with lemon mayonnaise."

"It's too cold for that," Waldo said. "I thought a rarebit. You have that funny electric-light look, as if you're catching something. That is, if you haven't already caught something. Cheers, and now I'll tell you what I bought Mrs. Donahue this morning."

His own call, which he made at least once daily, had been more successful. Irena had been still in bed and sounded it, warm, sleepy. "Yes, I'm all alone," a teasing soft laugh, "so we can talk, Waldo. By the way, I hope your being in constant communication doesn't mean snooping? I won't have that, you know . . ."

"All it means," Waldo said, "is that I can't get through a day without you."

He had always, in his contained way, owned himself emotionally and now was disturbed to find that this was no longer true.

An occasional glance at his watch by Waldo punctuated two leisurely drinks and the rarebit.

"I have to meet a man in a bar about a picture, at two-thirty. It's amazing how much business is done in this country over whiskey."

"And in New York over gin and vermouth," Celia said. "As long as you're going to dump me into the wet and cold, I will go and pay my respects to the Book of Kells, although I understand I only get to see one page of it, tied back with ribbon."

In the after-lunch exodus from hotels and restaurants she couldn't find a taxi, and hadn't acquainted herself with the routes taken by the tall blue buses. She walked in the heavy rain to the library of Trinity College and gave the ritual silently inspecting moments to the Book of Kells on its stand, following a straggling line and hearing people saying, "But only the one page . . . ?"

It was the library itself that delighted her: naved, with its upper balconies and corkscrewed graceful iron staircases. A solemn but reassuring cathedral of books.

Her wet chilled feet felt very far under her and she was beginning to have a slight dreamlike feeling which had nothing to do with lunchtime martinis. Lovely idea, go back to the hotel and have a nap while Waldo did his picture-dealing, and get rid of a cold or some unlikely bug before it bit in.

Waldo, a difficult and demanding patient himself, did not lightly brook other people's illnesses.

Bernard was waiting at the bar in a noisy pub on Talbot Street. To the left of him, a group of men were singing a song unfamiliar to Waldo, something about roses and donkeys, and a furious argument about football was going on on his other side.

Bernard lifted his large whiskey and gestured at a dim corner.

"We'll want privacy."

Waldo ordered himself a forbiddingly level-headed mineral water, ignored the bartender's gaze of astonishment, and carried his glass and bottle to the wooden bench, facing the loud activity of the bar but separated from it by a battered oak table and a great many hard-drinking backs.

The meeting had been arranged by Bernard over the telephone while Celia was in the shower after breakfast. Waldo had been calm, cold. "Fifteen minutes or so, no more, if that's what's needed to get you off our backs."

Bernard had treated himself to a new raincoat, which he had already given a severe rumpling. "Sit down, sit down," he cried hospitably, moving over on the cracked red leather cushion of the bench. "Lousy weather."

Waldo sat with a swift folding movement, sipped his water, and said, "What's it about?"

"My territory," Bernard began obliquely, "includes New Jersey, Connecticut, and lower New York although I have a few customers upstate. It's a funny business, you're run off your feet sometimes and then there'll be days when the appointments dry up. I had some time on my hands the last few weeks, Christmas parties and so on, the whole damned business more or less cranks to a halt until after they've dried out, after New Year's."

"And what," Waldo said, "did you do with your time?"

"I was dropping around one noon to ask you out for a bite and a friendly chat when I saw you and that girl, that blonde, flagging down a cab. I don't know, something about the way she looked at you and held your arm . . . anyway, just on a hunch I followed along, and then I kept it up as a kind of hobby. I mean, man, almost every day, you've really got it made, she's quite a . . ." He rolled his eyes upward.

No sign of Waldo's rage was visible. He took out a cigarette and flicked his lighter with a quiet hand.

"Lunch over at about one-fifteen, off around the corner to the yellow canopy and all tucked in until about two-fifteen, two-thirty, then separate cabs back, funny when you're both returning to the same place—"

"Are you through now?" Waldo asked. "I've heard your tale and I must go, I have a busy afternoon."

Bernard, red-faced with drink, eyes bulging in disbelief, gave him a lobster glare and said, "What the hell do you mean, you must go and am I through, I've just begun."

"Finish, then, in a sentence."

"Okay, a sentence. My fair share of the old bitch's estate. I worked my ass for it, I have every reason to expect it. Your wife as much as admits that, I'm only asking what's due me, another man would demand half. It's not only the house, but I know for a fact that there's valuable furniture there, a chair for instance, you'd think it was the throne of the Pope of Rome, the prices they get for these things. All I want is"—rapidly adjusting it upward for bargaining purposes—"thirty-five. I'd thought forty but let's be reasonable."

He added to himself, okay, twenty-five, he'd be doing nicely, even if by rights it was his property he was discussing. He felt magnanimous.

"You must live in a fantasy world," Waldo said. "If you're blackmailing me, forget it. If it's Celia you plan to approach with this information, forget that too. One, there's nothing in it. And two, she's quite comfortable with a lover of her own." He leaned forward and went on gently, "Any way you look at it, you're fucked dead in your tracks, Bernard."

His voice was so soft that this serene observation went unheard; but there were a great many witnesses to what followed.

Bernard's balloon did not collapse easily. He hurled the contents of his drink into Waldo's face and cried, panting, "There are other ways, other ways, I warn you I have a temper that lets go on me. Unless you do the fair thing, I might just wring your sonofabitching neck in some dark alley, how would you like that—or *hers*. I'm not to be played with by Sir Waldo St.

Clair, laughted at, made little of, you snide smooth lying bastard—and talking in that bloody way about my cousin, your
own wife—" He lunged forward and caught Waldo's neck between his big hands.

Even for a tolerant Irish pub, this was too much. A short,
heavily muscled man who had been drinking stout and idly
watching a few feet away from them tore Bernard's hands away
with surprising strength.

"I'm off duty," he said pleasantly, "but would you like to
charge the fellow?"

Waldo got to his feet, wiping his face with his handkerchief
and then rubbing the back of his hand across his throat. He
now had fascinated listeners. With a fine throwaway style that
drew the approval of his audience, he said:

"Thank you, but he's only"—light ironic smile, clear carrying
voice—"threatened to kill me or my wife or for all I know both
of us. He made as you saw a start on the project here, but I
wouldn't say it was quite the place for a successful murder. No,
drop it, he's a distant relative and we'll charitably say it was
only the drink. Or let's hope so. Speaking of drinks, officer, a
large whiskey for you and thank you very much. And with my
fingers crossed that there'll be another one of you around next
time we have a family meeting."

To the general approbation of the pub—"all combed and
brushed and curried, the fellow, but a cool customer, a tough
little chap underneath it all"—he paid for the policeman's
drink at the bar.

Then he walked composedly to the pegs by the door,
collected his raincoat and umbrella, and went out without so
much as a look over his shoulder at the savagely crouched man
on the cracked leather cushion, about to order another whiskey
and about to be summarily refused it.

CHAPTER 12

Through an increasing haze in her head, Celia walked a block from Trinity College, hesitated, then hailed a cab. Things to do, presents to buy, but not right now. Later.

Ridiculous . . . you can't catch a cold a few hours after getting your feet wet in the rain; it has to settle in and incubate. Perhaps that enormous man on the plane, elbow in her lap, sleeping almost on her shoulder, had passed it along to her as a fringe benefit of his company, and the Dublin weather had merely served to bring the germ into bloom.

In any case, there was nothing to do but deal with it directly, get rid of it, before Waldo began by looking patient and martyred and then started scolding.

It was an added weariness to see the packages someone had neatly stacked on the writing desk in the sitting room. Christmas bounty mailed to them. She had dealt with her list before leaving New York, but there were always those people who gave you a first-time unexpected gift and sent you into a minor panic.

Of course, there couldn't be—yes, there was. She recognized the firm crisp printing and the return address in the corner and held the package in her hands a few moments before she opened it. A copy of *Pride and Prejudice*, one of her cherished books, read ritually every three years, although she couldn't remember telling him about that. Bound in silk-soft emerald green calf, a slim light volume, pages brilliantly edged in gold, end papers marbled in peacock colors, and in his hand on the flyleaf, "Celia from Cy."

Nothing else. What else could he write in a book that other hands might pick up and leaf through?

Of course, he would have had to send something to Waldo too, and there it was, looking in its wrappings very much like another book.

A book makes a nice impersonal present.

She soaked in a deep bath, took aspirin, and went to bed with *Pride and Prejudice*. The haze thickened. The tulips on the curtains floated, came near, receded. Rain swept the windows, making a rushing music. Book open, under her hand, she went off into a heavy sleep.

Waldo found her still sleeping when he came in after four. He went over the the bed and stood looking down at her, hands hanging quietly at his side. The helplessness of sleep, the mystery of it, she could be in China or back at the age of three, or with Cy Hall, wandering in some delightful place . . .

He saw the book under her hand, gently extracted it, read the inscription, riffled lightly through the petal-thin pages, turned it upside down and gave it a little shake; and then replaced it on the bed, near her hand.

The slight motion, the presence over her woke her and she looked up into his face as if wondering who he was and then shot upright.

"You scared me—" Eyes wide, unfocused for a second.

"Expecting someone else?" Dry amused voice. "And me playing Santa Claus for you—"

She saw the heap of packages he had dumped on his bed, little ones, large ones. Oh God, she'd lost a day somewhere, tomorrow was his birthday, she'd almost forgotten the landmark birthday, and the day after was Christmas Eve; she had no idea of the business hours of Dublin shops on Christmas Eve. Early closing, maybe. And there was only one present for the two celebrations so far, the hacking jacket.

She told herself that the sleep had done her a great deal of good. Time to get down to business. Wasn't there a theory

that people contract colds because they refuse to cope? She
seized on the encouraging demanding little word.

Cope.

He looked thoughtfully at her as she got out of bed. "You're
appealingly pink—you're not getting a cold?"

"A little one, I put it to bed, I think it's almost gone—" Her
voice was slightly hoarse.

"Then you're not up to Canavan House this evening?"

"Canavan House?"

"A tea and sherry reception we've been invited to, very
grand, he's in Parliament—the Dail I suppose—and she col-
lects young artists, Mrs. D. gave me a note to her."

"No, I don't want to go around possibly infecting hundreds,
and I have things to buy—" She gave another look at the pile
on his bed. There must be a dozen presents, and they must be
all for her.

"I'll order up some hot tea. That and a couple of my cold
tablets should put you back on your feet."

Waiting for their tea, he changed his wet clothes and put on
a severely handsome black suit, white shirt, dark glowing amber
tie.

Taking her cold pills obediently, with a hope they wouldn't
quarrel with the aspirin, she said, "You look a little strange
yourself, pale—"

"Pre-birthday sinking sensations," Waldo said. "Don't be
surprised if I arrive home late and tipsy, I'll be having the last
fling of my thirties. What exactly are your plans?"

"I'll have tea and dress and then go out, the stores are open
late at least tonight. And I am sorry, Waldo, I should be going
with you but I've got to catch up with myself and time is running out."

Staring at her, he said, "It's only a birthday after all and
Christmas, not the apocalypse. Don't overdo it if you're feeling
rocky."

He, not she, was the one who needed sympathy and a lift of

morale now. "I'm feeling fine." A little giddy and unreal, and
hot. Surely not a fever. Cope.

Tea arrived; Waldo downed a quick cup and put on his
black trenchcoat, which he referred to as my villainous one as
against the oyster-white Burberry.

The desk called a few moments after the door closed behind
him. "Mr. St. Clair forgot to leave you the address and telephone number of Canavan House where he's off to, have you a
pencil handy?"

When she went out the rain had thinned, but this time she
was booted and prepared, warm and dry inside her yellow coat.

The feeling of unreality persisted.

The eyes of shop assistants looked overlarge but their voices
were curiously remote and far away. If only there weren't so
many people, normally polite people, now hurrying, pushing.

On Nassau Street, she bought Waldo two handkerchief
linen shirts, one pale tangerine and one lilac, and three wool
ties in interesting plaids. A beginning, but there was that awful
heap of his to meet, to match.

Might as well face Grafton Street, where the big stores and
the big crowds were. Umbrellas tangled with umbrellas; you
had to pick your way step by step along the sidewalk. Gloves
there, to her left. She bought a pair, of heavy cable-crocheted
creamy wool.

A man was selling oranges right outside the shop. Someone
jolted his tray and he howled imprecations as oranges rolled,
hands gleefully snatched. Celia tripped on an orange and almost fell.

Buses towering and lurching by, so close, cars weaving, no
rhyme or reason to the traffic flow, and in the shifting flare of
light people darting every which way across the street, didn't
they care whether they lived or died? Perhaps in this Catholic
republic the next world was more appealing.

And the noise, the horns, the cries echoing through her head,
a cluster of shabby children with tambourines singing "Adeste
Fideles," a man deep in drink shouting, "Down with the

Pope!" Another cry, "Shame on you, shame!" as the female admonisher's shopping bag was thwacked hard against his knees. Jeaned boys, a group of them, with long soaked hair, playing some kind of game, chasing each other down the street, cutting through people like cars through traffic; a shoulder hit hers, and she caught at a lamppost for support.

Birthday presents *and* Christmas presents, you've only begun. Press on, Celia. Silver cufflinks, shaped and studded like starfish. A slender little gold-plated clothespin to clip to a tie. He could use another cigarette case; she bought one in tobacco brown morocco. Turning to leave the shop, she hesitated inside its glass door, looking out at the rain, the river of umbrellaed bodies.

Another hour or less ought to do it, spend a little more time and pile up some more packages on this madhouse thoroughfare and then retreat to the relative quiet of Dawson Street for books and records.

She forced herself out into the stream. It seemed, in this peculiar evening, not at all unnatural that the red-headed tinker woman should come face to face with her under a streetlight, her child still slung damply over her hip. This time she too had an umbrella. She made a fierce near-swipe with it at Celia.

"*You.* I see you haven't broken your leg yet, but give you time, and no amount of money will buy the curse off you now—"

"Be off, Belinda, leave the lady alone," a man said behind her, clapping a hand on the ragged shoulder. "And mind where you spit!" She must be known, in Dublin. Waldo said it was a parochial town, and that if you sneezed in the Four Courts they'd bless you in Merrion Square.

The encounter lent an edge of doom to the darkness. She had a momentary impulse to burst into tears. I feel so awful, and here's this woman spitting at me, and I must get across the street somehow—yes, thank God, a traffic light.

She waited dizzily at the curb for the light to change. The

motion, the pressure behind her was frightening, people three
or four deep like a great wave impatient to break.

A bus passed a foot from her nose and knocked her umbrella
back. Someone shrieked, "You'll have my eye out!"

And then there was the object at the small of her back, and
the savage push forward. The light hadn't changed. Not fifteen
yards away there were the great white blinding eyes of a moving bus.

In a period of split seconds impossibly slowed, eternal, she
felt herself toppling forward, thought she heard herself screaming, or was it someone else.

Before the mind, in the face of the unfaceable, turned itself
off, she found herself thinking among a dozen other long, long
thoughts, I've caught my death, I've caught my death.

And, My *presents*—

Cy, oh Cy.

It hit her, death, it must be, a great midair springing, a hur-
tling, face to face, but a body, what a strange feeling, bones,
flesh, impact, cruel, hurting, where were the headlights, the
steel, the screaming rubber, the tearing horns—?

"God have mercy on us, the creature's dead." "Drunk, was
she, I saw her swaying, like—" "No, not dead, don't you see
the lashes moving, so?" "For God's sake get a policeman."
"And her pretty packages all scattered, here, this one, and this
one—" "The great gossoon, dashing over here against the light,
he slammed right into her, he trying to get out from under the
bus wheels before they hit him . . . and just picked himself up
and off with him, never stopped to see what he'd done . . ."
"Well, in a way, lucky for her, d'you think she was wanting to
do away with herself? Jumping forward like that, the bus coming—"

Celia heard portions of it in a half faint, not quite believing
she was alive, not quite ready to acknowledge the impossible
and beautiful, the miraculous.

Extinction one second, and in the next her head against the

wet cold pavement, a great stunned cloudiness, and voices poking into the cloud from high above.

Rain, feelable rain, bouncing off the toe of an elegant withdrawing black shoe inches from her eyes tickled her cheek. Moons of bending faces, helpful hands reaching down to her. A fat man knelt and put an arm under her shoulders.

"Stand back, what's all this?"

A young policeman lifted her to her feet and was bombarded with a dozen theories. He shook his head impatiently as if disposing of gnats.

These people, paying no attention whatever to the lights, taking their lives into their hands; he gathered that the good God had sent her another such a damned fool as herself flying from the opposite side of the street, just in the nick of time.

He felt her begin to shake. She reached for her eyes and said, "My glasses—"

"Here, miss, thanks to the Holy Mother they weren't stepped on, and I've gathered up your packages, a bit wet and muddy but—"

Celia could have wept at the kindness of the dumpy woman with the purple birthmarked forehead.

Her intelligence was not yet functioning. She was totally occupied in being alive.

"Will you be wanting a doctor? Have you cut yourself or hurt your head?" the policeman asked, still supporting her firmly.

"No, just the shock—the scare and the fall," her own voice almost unrecognizable to her. "If I could get a cab to the Shelbourne—" Her knees buckled and he tightened his hold.

"I don't think your legs are up to getting you home alone any way at all," he said. "Here, take a step. And another. That's a good girl. Blossom by blossom the spring begins." What a delightful policeman to find, in a world magically given back to her. "Cab there! In we go, the two of us. The Shelbourne, and mind your driving, this lady's had enough of fair Dublin's traffic."

Cy Hall had called from Dublin Airport. The St. Clairs' room didn't answer. He went through Customs, got a Mercedes taxi and had himself driven to their hotel. His driver, who was loquacious, gestured at the American Consulate as they passed it. "We call it the Crown of Thorns. The architecture, you'll understand, not the intent. And are you familiar with the bird market, sir? Poor souls in cages, it'd make you bleed to see them bottled up. Now the canal here was once a thriving waterway . . ."

The lobby of the Shelbourne was festive. Well-dressed people hurried in and out to pleasure, a holiday kind of expectancy in their faces. Christmas decorations sparkled discreetly. From the left, from the right, came the delightful lark notes of the page boys, "*Mis*-tah Crevass, Mis-tah Crevass . . . Mis-tah Schmidt, *Mis*-tah Schmidt," the name Schmidt taking on a high unlikely music.

Thinking that at any minute he might see Celia, he felt a little as he had at the age of three when he had first gazed upon, with full comprehension, the Christmas tree in the library.

Celia with her brown hair and her glasses, her candles all lit for him.

The girl at the desk said, "Their room doesn't answer? Perhaps they're napping, but I have the impression they haven't come back yet, I believe they went out separately. Just a minute—I have an address and a telephone number where Mr. St. Clair can be reached, as a matter of fact I just gave it out to someone else, he's a popular man tonight—"

"No," Cy said, "it's Mrs. St. Clair I want," and fought the smile that at any second could turn into runaway laughter.

He cast an eye at the bar but resisted its lure; he might miss her– What impossible good luck, their having gone their separate ways when leaving the hotel, if she came in alone.

He stood near the door, willing her to him out of the dark outside. When she came, she was not alone, but accompanied by a policeman and immediately the object of fascinated stares.

The gay yellow raincoat smeared and dirty, hair tossed, an air of emotional dishevelment—he thought for a wild moment that she was unaccountably and thoroughly drunk.

She saw him and before she could stop herself cried out his name on a long piercing gasp.

CHAPTER 13

"Mr. St. Clair?" the policeman asked.

"No—Celia, what's happened—?"

"This lady had a close shave, just missed a bad street accident, so I though I'd see her safe back to home and mother as it were." The policeman was puzzled; like most people, he was susceptible to love, and he felt in the air about him a heat and a startling sweetness.

"If you're a friend then, I'll give her into your keeping, I've got to get back." Celia tried brokenly to thank him; he waved it off and said over his shoulder as he left them, "A life saved is a fine present to everybody."

Before a vastly intrigued international audience, the man ("Yes, quite attractive, really") put an arm about the untidy woman (It must have been a *lovely* party!") and said firmly and gently, as tears began pouring down her face,

"Don't cry, darling, don't cry, love, or at least not here, hold off if you can—have you got your key or is it at the desk?"

It was in her pocket. She handed it to him and fumbled for paper tissues in her handbag as her nose began to run. What a vision she must be, to him. Aftershock licked nearer, hysteria threatened, but the arm around her in the elevator and then in the long Persian-carpeted corridor clasped her so tightly it almost hurt. She concentrated on the arm. Cy's arm, appearing from nowhere in the middle of darkness, disaster.

Inside the door, he flicked on lights. She saw herself with horror in a mirror and ran a hand over her tumbled hair. Dirt on her cheek, the cheek of a ghastly torn-apart face.

"I have to—"

"Go ahead. I'll order brandy. And I won't have you crying behind a closed door, please don't, and before you go away and put yourself back together—" He put both arms around her and held her against him and said over and over, "It's all right, Celia," until she stopped trembling.

He waited in the sitting room for a very long five minutes. She came back washed, brushed, and desperately pale.

"Drink first. Explanations later." He handed her the little balloon glass of brandy and touched his frosty martini to its edge. "Try to get it all down and then I'll give you a refill."

The brandy was searing and steadying.

"I don't understand, first the nightmare and then the fairy tale," she said, color beginning to come back to her face. "Where did you come from, Cy? I mean, how on earth was it that you were there, right there, just when I . . ."

"We'll get to that. What about the near accident?"

It was all mixed up in her head and came out disconnectedly, the rain, and tripping over a rolling orange, the tinker woman, pursuing her curse, spitting, the buses so hair-raisingly close to the curbs, the umbrellas that made it difficult to see around you, behind you—

And then she broke off and stared at him as it came back to her with the impact of a blow across the heart.

"Someone tried to kill me."

It was said not to him but to the air around her, her voice distant, stunned.

"Celia darling . . . you've been pushed and shoved in crowds before at God knows how many New York street corners—"

"In the small of my back, something, maybe the tip of an umbrella or the edge of an attache case, or a man's or a woman's cane . . . hard to tell exactly, through the coat and my suit jacket underneath . . . but it didn't feel accidental, it felt directed, it felt, what's the word, *personal*, and vicious . . ."

The endless seconds of terror as she fell forward caught her up again; she gripped her hands tightly together, against her breasts, looking back at the seconds, looking back at the toppling body, doomed.

". . . and then some madman tried to make it against the light from the other side of the street and slammed straight into me and knocked me flat on the sidewalk, and . . . saved my life . . ."

He was sitting beside her on the little silk-covered sofa. He would very much like to have had her in his arms but there were after all two legal inhabitants of this suite.

"Let me have your glass, and then we'll think about food." Calm, soothing voice.

She thought she heard the unsaid words, My poor Celia, temporarily around the bend, so scared out of her wits that now she's having delusions of persecution, attempted murder.

Giving her back her glass, he went on in a child-quieting way, "Who in any case do you think would want to kill you?"

"I haven't the faintest idea, unless Bernard—but that's mad, I have a feeling he's all noise and bluster, except when his temper takes over. This wasn't temper. This was deliberate. I think."

But the certainty had left her voice and her eyes, in the face of his kind, concerned disbelief. Keep talking, talk it out of her system, bury it, forget it. Helped along by him.

"I suppose it *could* have been something accidental, meaningless? Someone just out of a shop trying to get an umbrella open, and jostled by someone else, and the thing catching me in the back, you do make a hard shoving movement when you open an umbrella—"

"And what's this about Bernard? Yes, you're probably right, about the umbrella."

"He's followed us here like a limpet, he wants a share in that damned house in Philadelphia and he wants it in a hurry. Just to dot the i's, he might have some wild idea that it would come to him as next of kin, blood relatives he called it, when I was flattened out under a bus. Not knowing that I'd willed everything I'd die possessed of to Waldo—people are awfully igno-

rant about property, I know I am—he might have a court case
that would stand up with me dead—"

Waldo or no Waldo, he took her in his arms and kissed her
with possessive passion and out of the long silence finally said,
"That's enough, Celia. Flattened. *Wills*. Dead. Go out and
come back in by another door and start all over again. You had
a lucky escape from an accident but you made it, you're sound
in wind and limb, and you're about to consume a good and
nourishing dinner if I have any say in the matter."

He finished his drink, released her very slowly and reluc-
tantly, and stood up. "I think on the whole we'd be better
downstairs in the grill. If your legs will hold you up. I don't
think I'd be good at French farce and anyway it's almost impossible to keep my hands off you . . . Enter Waldo. 'And
what are you doing here, Cy?' 'Oh, just a little dinner for two
in your rooms . . .' "

Smiling shakily, warm from his arms, she said, "And what, to
return to it, are you doing here, Cy?"

"I'm on my way to a Reynolds or so in Aberdeen. Sir Joshua
that is. I knew it was ill-advised and imprudent and all the rest
of it but I couldn't be this near and not try to see you."

"How long, then, do I have of you?"

"I'm booked to leave mid-morning tomorrow." He reached
for the phone and ordered another martini to drink while she
changed out of her damp clothes. Annoyed and amused at himself, he picked up a defensive copy of the *Irish Times* from the
arm of a chair and settled with it held wide.

Oh hello, Waldo, just catching up with the *Times* while
Celia gets her clothes on— A man deep in his newspaper wears
a certain air of innocent detachment.

They went down to the grill, found a corner booth, and had
dinner, which took rather a long time as Celia had trouble at
first getting it down. On command, she went carefully through
a cup of consommé, a cheese omelet, a roll and butter, and a
small dish of vanilla ice cream. Cy hungrily but absent-mindedly ate steak and duchess potatoes and an anchovy and
asparagus salad washed down with Guinness.

He held out the glass to her. "Take a sip of this. It's strengthening, they say."

Not wanting it but understanding the shared glass, she drank a little.

Now that she had stopped obsessively talking about what had happened to her, he found himself appalled at the near miss. Celia. Destroyed bloody bundle in a yellow raincoat. Sirens, ambulances, sorry, too late. A tiny news item at the bottom of a column, American Woman Dies in Grafton Street Traffic Accident.

With sudden fierce and illogical indignation, he said, "Where the hell was Waldo while you were wandering around being cursed and falling over oranges and all but under wheels?"

"At a reception at a place called Canavan House, I didn't want to go because I'd caught a cold, dear God I hope I haven't given it to you—"

"I'd rather have yours than anybody else's and for some reason I don't get them. Yes, Molly Canavan. She sent us Mrs. Donahue. In that connection, I couldn't help wondering—Mrs. D. came into the gallery early this week looking for Waldo, and was surprised he'd gone off at this time of year." He buttered a piece of brown bread. "She said she'd told him there was no hurry for her pictures—the apartment won't be ready until May."

Celia found this odd, Waldo having given her the impression that he must get about the Donahue business immediately. But, in a lassitude of delivery, of love, she contented herself with looking across the table at him, cherishing the shape of his mouth and the texture of his eyebrows.

"*Miss*-iss St. Clair!" warbled a page boy at the entrance to the grill as they were finishing their coffee. "Miss-iss St. *Clair*."

She got up and went to a phone in the lobby while Cy paid the bill. Waldo, who else?

"Hello—"

Click. A dead line. The page boy must have got it wrong. Either that or someone was trying to satisfy himself that she was there, at the hotel.

Behind her, Cy said, "I'll take you up and bid you good night and," casually, "say hello to Waldo if he surfaces."

She was braced, half-expecting to see him when she unlocked the door. The lighted rooms proclaimed their serene emptiness.

"Well, love." He stood looking down at her, committing her, the way she was just now, to memory.

She reached out and touched his sleeve. "Just making sure, once again, it's really you, and you're really here, I'm not having a dream with my head on the sidewalk—"

He took the doubting hand in both of his.

". . . When I was told you were in Paris, I had you all fixed up with a girl named Amélie whom you always spend your Christmases with . . ."

"My Christmases in future," he said, "will always be spent with a girl named Celia. As well as the rest of my year. I hope by now we understand each other?" His eyes were near and steady, demanding an answer.

Her eyes, lost in his, said it before she spoke. "Yes, Cy, yes, we do."

To the flicking sound of a key, the door opened.

"Well, good evening," Waldo said. "Pleasant surprise, Cy."

"Waldo—"

His head was heavily, dramatically bandaged. Blood stained his shirt collar.

He walked slowly to the vacated sofa and collapsed on it and said, "Who will be the first to pour a brandy for the walking wounded?"

CHAPTER 14

Bernard waited in the rain outside Canavan House with what
was, for him, patience. Striding the block from end to end, but
keeping close to the house walls so he couldn't be spotted from
a window; lighting one cigarette from the end of another; and
cursing to himself at the rain and the chill.

When he had called the Shelbourne, asking for Mr. St.
Clair, the girl said in a holding-back way, "You aren't Mr.
Caldwell by any chance?" Slippery little bastard, thinking it
was as simple as that, that he was a fly to be swatted away.
"No," he said instantly, "I'm Moran." He got the address.

An umbrella would have been hampering but he wished he
had one. He thought with longing of the cosy place on Banquet Street. Slummy-looking alley but nice setup she had, fireplace and all. He had had a semi-sobering huge tea there, his
toast browned for him on a fork held out to the fire.

They had met at a pub near his hotel the night before, fallen
into the conversation of the lonely, taken immediately to each
other and at closing time parted fast friends. "Next time," Bernard said, "I won't let you go home alone, that I promise you."

She was a big, tall woman, pink and white, heavy-breasted,
with thick dark hair worn the way his mother had worn hers, in
a great loose Psyche knot which she absent-mindedly kept pat-
ting and pinning at just as his mother had done. Her blue eyes
were large, kind, and gullible.

She was a masseuse, she told him, at which Bernard winked,
but then he found she was perfectly in earnest. "Lovely job,
hard work in its way but my time's my own, I come and go as I

like, only women of course, dear, the men in this country are shy . . ."

Bernard assured her that he wouldn't be shy.

At teatime, he went over his grievances again with her, bathing himself in her ready sympathy.

". . . burned up my letter, had the gall to laugh in my face when I brought up the matter of his girlfriend . . ."

"A grand big fellow like you doesn't have to take lip from anybody," Doreen McGrath said. "Have another cream cake, do."

As she got the story, they were holding back money they owed him, a great deal of money, from property left to him and the cousin. She herself was a member of a large contentious family and not only believed him implicitly but was wholly on his side. Going off to sleep after parting with him last night, she had allowed herself to think that maybe the loneliness was over, somewhere in the future a ring, and the title Mrs. to gloat over. And the States, she'd always wanted to go to the States. A bit beforehand, perhaps, but they'd gotten on beautifully from the first hesitant hello . . .

". . . not only the house itself on one of the best streets in Philadelphia, but several pieces of valuable furniture, and a pile of jewelry, diamonds, and so on . . . and just the other day I remembered my mother talking about a collection of antique silver she had in a corner cabinet in the dining room, but all I ever saw was old yellow newspaper inside the panes . . ."

Her womanly attention to his comfort, her warm blue gaze, gave him a heady feeling of capability, of strength.

"What the fellow wants is a show of force, a touch of the fist to give him an idea who he's dealing with," he said through his cream cake. "He's half the size I am. Thinks you can do your business with your tongue and that's all there is to it."

Canavan House was number thirteen. Correctly numbered all right, Bernard said to himself. Some kind of pale stone, big place, purple door at the top of a wide shallow flight of slate steps, great tall windows, filmy lacy stuff and what looked like red velvet, a starry chandelier, moving heads and shoulders.

Waldo probably warming himself, glass in hand, at some roaring fire while his cousin-in-law waited in the rain . . .

Waldo sauntering out of the pub this afternoon, leaving him crouched and momentarily beaten because of the bloody policeman at his elbow, Waldo looking as if he owned the world. With my fingers crossed, officer, that there'll be another of you around the next time we have a family meeting.

Well, there was no one to speak of around, police or otherwise. The crowds, the stores, were blocks away. This was the time, on this kind of street, to be at home, sheltered, happy, safe, and rich.

Waldo was a little drunk when he left Canavan House, but erect and graceful about it. He walked south on Merrion Street and turned in at a corner gate to St. Stephen's Green. Passing close to the immense bulk and towering gloom of a yew tree, he was seized from behind in an iron grip. A large hand clapped itself over his mouth and jaw.

"I meant it, you know, about the dark alley," Bernard said, breath hot on Waldo's skin, voice low and whiskied. "You won't listen to reason, you won't listen to right and justice, maybe you'll listen to force. Don't move or try to call out, I have the point of my knife at the back of your neck"—a delicate proving prick at the nape—"but I'm not going to kill you. Yet. I will, though, unless you come through, and fast, and you'll never know when or where it's coming from, your death—"

Footsteps neared. Dark as it was, Bernard pulled Waldo to the far side of the yew tree. His prey was very still, the tiny cold knifepoint reminding him to be so; animal-quiet, braced.

"I'll be in touch with you tomorrow sometime, you'll be back in business by then, but just to let you know I'm a man of my word, and not to be pushed around and laughed away—"

Waldo, suddenly released and beginning to turn, got a stunning blow behind the ear and crashed forward against the tree bole, hung there for a moment, and fell sprawling to the grass.

A boy and a girl, the tree their trysting place rain or shine, day or night, found him there unconscious a few minutes later.

"Drunk is it?" the boy said. "He's cut his head, look at the blood will you. A robbery maybe"—he searched and found the American word—"a mugging." Excited and important, he told his girl to run to the far corner and bring a policeman. "And hurry. He looks bad, I'll just take a handkerchief to the blood."

Waldo whirled brandy in his glass. "Fortunately, there was a doctor around the corner, he got me X-rayed and stitched up, only a flesh wound where I hit the tree. Your cousin knows exactly the spot, behind the ear, to go for, he was very artistic about it."

He was telling his tale with a certain relish, as though it had happened to someone else. Taken aback at his manner, Celia explained to herself that he was still lightheaded, probably, and perhaps a little drunk after the Canavan House festivities; and then, he responded to drama in any form.

While she listened to him, a voice in another part of her mind asked, had he heard them before he came in? *All my Christmases . . . Yes, Cy, oh yes . . .*

He gave no sign of it if he had.

"Congratulations on your aplomb, Waldo," Cy said crisply. "Anyone would think you got knocked on the head as a regular thing, you take it so well in stride." He was standing in front of the fire, his face intent and sharply worried. "What the hell are you going to do about this madman? Suppose he goes after Celia next? Of course you brought the police up to date on him?"

"I was in no shape, my knees giving under me, to go and make a formal charge at a police station, and answer four hundred and three plodding questions. In any case the doctor ordered me home and to bed. I gave my policeman Bernard's name and description, told him I didn't know what hotel he's staying in but it's somewhere off O'Connell Street. The trouble is, there were no witnesses and I think he detected a strong recollection of John Jameson on my breath. Besides, family fists used against each other aren't all that unheard-of in this country."

"Correction—you're not taking it in stride after all, you sound slightly deranged yourself," Cy said. "Giving the matter the back of your hand— Celia had a rough evening too. She thought someone tried to push her under a bus on Grafton Street. I thought she was crazy. Now I'm not so sure."

Waldo raised a hand to his bandaged head. He looked, for all his jauntiness, on a dangerous brink, bones etched sharply against the pallor of his face; his hand shook.

"A bus—"

"We've had enough horrors," Celia said. "I'm here, I'm safe, and I'm not sure any more, not sure of anything—"

At her rising voice Cy, before he could stop himself, put a steadying hand on her shoulder.

"Poor Cy, *two* battered St. Clairs to comfort all in the one night," Waldo said. "By the way, have you come three thousand miles because it's my birthday tomorrow? I take that as a great courtesy." His smile had a faintly Cheshire cat look.

"I'm more or less on business, as you are. Happy birthday anyway. To get back to your cousin—"

"Not mine. Celia's, thank God. Well, I'll hasten to try and reassure you, I've got to get this head on its pillow. With luck the police will call around the hotels tonight, try to track him down, see if there really is a Bernard Caldwell and I haven't invented him out of the mists of alcohol. If they find out where he's staying, I will go and see him tomorrow morning—accompanied by a police escort—and have what I plan to be a final interview with him."

"You don't think," Cy said slowly, "you could give in to nice comfortable cowardice—for both of you—and take Celia home? No point in Caldwell's staying here after you leave. He has a job back there, an address, a phone number, he can be got at and taken care of by suitable authorities if he tries anything else."

Waldo yawned. "We'll see how my interview goes. And if you don't mind my saying so, I think you should take your*self* home, I've had it and Celia looks as if she has too. If you have another home, that is. Maybe you're in the next room here for all I know."

"The Gresham," Cy said, picking up his raincoat. "I'll call you in the morning, Waldo, before I leave, to see what you've arranged. I'm concerned even if you're not."

"Yes, daddy," Waldo said. "It's a great relief to have someone bandying orders about and seeing to our safety, Celia's and mine."

Doreen had a great fragrant lamb stew all but ready for him. She was industriously skimming the fat from its surface when he came in, his swagger restored to him.

He went over and gave her a domestic kiss and sniffed the stew with great pleasure.

"Out cold," he said, "in that Stephen's Park, or whatever it is. No permanent harm, maybe a stiff neck tomorrow."

She gave him a look of admiration mixed with apprehension. She had vivid recollections of a family lawsuit concerning the ownership of a bull, the verdict followed by near-broken heads, and policemen.

"You don't think he might charge you? You wouldn't want the police after you, they might cramp your style."

"I was thinking about that on the way back—uh—home, here." He put an arm around her waist and hugged her to him. "I thought I might change hotels and give a fake name but that won't work, have to show your passport . . ."

Shyly she said, "Not to put myself forward, I can give you shelter for a night or two, and then, I have a cousin runs a rooming house out in Ballsbridge, just outside the city, she wouldn't give a damn about names or passports."

She was rewarded with a hearty kiss. "You're a pal, Doreen. It's not that I'm afraid of anything the little bastard could do to get back at me, but I want to get on with my arrangements. Let's have a drink before your stew."

She poured whiskey for the two of them. "And you really think he'll be knocked back to his senses now, let you have what's by rights coming to you?"

"I think there's a good chance, nothing like letting a man know you have to be dealt with, not shoved aside. And by the way, there's someone in your chair who might cash in a little too." Warmed with whiskey, the smell of stew, the partisanship of Doreen and the remembered releasing pleasure of his fist against bone, he felt generous and triumphant.

"I'll give him a call in the morning, set up a little business meeting with him and Celia. And if he isn't ready, then, to cooperate"—he took a large thirsty gulp of his drink—"I'll play my ace."

CHAPTER 15

"Happy birthday, Waldo."

She gave him, recklessly and guiltily, everything she had bought for his birthday and for Christmas. At six o'clock, she had gotten out tissue paper, fawn, brown, and cream, and spools of yellow and white satin ribbon, and wrapped his packages.

He was responsible for her early waking. She had been curled into the small sofa in the sitting room, under a pink blanket. Inching out of a bad dream, she was aware of lamplight, a face near, curiously dark under something strange and white, a pierce of eyes into her own. There was a clap of terror at her heart and then the darkness and the whiteness became Waldo, bandaged, yes, struck in the head, beaten about while she sat in a trance of love at a grillroom table—

"What are you doing out here?" he demanded softly.

"I started sneezing some time in the night . . . I thought I'd wake you and that you badly needed your sleep—"

She wondered how long he had been sitting on the arm of the sofa, watching her.

"Get back to bed, Waldo. How's your head?"

"Too many things going around in it," Waldo said, his gaze still deep in hers. "But birthdays aren't the time to talk about walls falling down on you."

Certainties wavered; the unreality which had started in the Aer Lingus plane caught her up again. She backed mentally away from it: Cy and the implicit promise she had made him.

Divorce.

Here in the black night-morning, it seemed an impossible,

mad scheme. With Waldo hurting physically and psychologically, ticking off the new number, forty, to himself, and talking of walls falling.

Before they had gone to sleep last night, he had her go step by step through her own calamitous evening.

At the end, he said, "It sounds too wild to be true, it was probably an accident, a coincidence, but seeing what a nut case Bernard is— Think back, Celia. You have an uncanny sense of smell. He reeks of tobacco, whiskey, and some kind of awful musk scent he must use by the bucket. He'd have been an arm's or umbrella's length behind you—"

She instinctively sniffed a little of the bedroom's warm safe air. "You'd make a good detective, Waldo . . . no, all I get is a trampled-on orange and wet wool. And sweat, unidentifiable as male or female."

Turning her head on the pillow, she had added after a moment's hesitation, "You don't think it would be wiser to give in, get rid of him? I don't know how much more either of us can take of this kind of thing."

Waldo snapped off the light. "Now you're sounding like the one with near-concussion. He wants thirty-five thousand dollars."

Unanswerable, of course.

He was opening his presents between bites of breakfast when the phone rang.

He said, "Dracula, probably—I'll get it."

It wasn't Bernard, but a polite cheerful police voice. "We found your bird, sir, or rather his nest but unfortunately he's flown away from it. He was staying at the Saint Basil, a run-down class of place on Cavendish Street. He checked out last evening at nine or a little later. So that's that. Is all quiet? Have you had any more trouble with your—er—relative?"

"No, but there's a possibility he tried to push my wife under a bus before he got around to me, one of your men very kindly saw her back to the hotel, there may be a report on it."

After a startled pause, the voice said tolerantly, "All's well that ends well—Merry Christmas to you, and of course you'll let us know if there are any more developments."

"Maddening," Waldo said to Celia. He sat down and opened another package. "Oh, what nice gloves," immediately trying them on. "Under the circumstances it was obliging of them to look for him at all. I suppose it's because we're visitors, Americans. Family quarrels in the streets of Dublin. Domestic disturbances. Their daily bread."

"Maybe he's given up and gone home. Money running out—"

"I heartily pray you're right," Waldo said, and, "I really have you trained in the matter of ties, these are terrific."

He was in his bath when the phone rang again.

Oh Cy darling, what am I going to say to you?

A woman's voice, lightly accented, identified itself as that of Irena Tova.

"Mrs. St. Clair? I'm terribly sorry to bother you at this hour but something's come up at the gallery, did yesterday rather, and I must talk to Waldo about it. I wanted to catch him before you went out."

Almost ten o'clock here, Celia though, almost five o'clock in New York. Conscientious of Irena Tova, very. She put her head in at the bathroom door. "New York for you. Irena."

Toweled and dripping, soap froth lacy on his sleek olive back, Waldo went to the telephone by the bed. She took the *Irish Times* off her own bed and went into the sitting room, trying to make the tactful retreat a casual matter.

He made no attempt to keep his voice down. "Good morning, Irena Katrina . . . well, thanks, but it's officially my very last birthday . . ." A long silence, and then, "About the Stella, things being the way they are, I'd be inclined to say go ahead, but see if you can pull him up five thousand higher, say you have another offer and you'll need twenty-four hours to check . . . yes, Irena Katrina, the same, exactly the same, here . . . Goodbye . . ."

Busy splashing sounds from the tub, and after a little while he came out dressed, glistening.

"Did you hear me step on my own grave, telling Irena it was my last birthday?" he asked, giving her a face-reading look.

"Yes, but I know what you mean . . . shall I order up more coffee for us?"

"You can't wash away ripe age with coffee, but . . . on the other hand I think I might manage a glass of champagne. Just as a way of saying the hell with it."

Or just as a way of celebrating a birthday call from Irena.

They were sitting on the little sofa sharing the champagne, Celia trying for gaiety, when the telephone burring at his elbow caught Waldo in mid-swallow.

It was Bernard. Celia heard, from several feet away, almost every word of the incredible conversation.

Polite, mildly concerned voice at first. "Feeling okay this morning, I hope?"

"Fine, thank you." Waldo sounding at his most dangerous, soft and icy. "Where are you calling from, by the way? The police would be interested."

"Like they say, that's for me to know and you to find out. But to get down to business, are you ready to have a little talk, you and Celia, get this thing wrapped up, over and done with?"

"Once and for all, you can take your murderous blackmail and shove it," Waldo said. "The answer is no. No. And in case you didn't hear me correctly . . . *no*."

"Oh well, too bad. I hoped I wouldn't have to go through with it, it's my property as well as yours, my loss as well as yours."

"Meaning what?"

"I thought you might see reason, I thought Celia might be able to persuade you, nine chances out of ten—but I took care of the tenth chance."

Casually, "And how did you go about that?"

"I have some friends in South Philly who I suppose you wouldn't call exactly respectable. It's all arranged that if and when they get the word from me over Ma Bell"—a brief relishing pause—"Miss Laura Gore's residence will be burned to the ground. They're good at it."

Celia, worried about Waldo's color—how could olive skin go mauve?—took his free hand in hers. It was cold and damp.

"Too bad all the old soul's goodies, that furniture, and the diamonds and rubies and things, have to be kissed goodbye along with the rest of the house, but there you are. And don't rub your hands over the insurance, she always raised hell over the premiums and got her coverage lowered, I remember the year before last she'd cut it to twenty-five thousand. To tell you the truth, I don't think she gave a damn about the house, and everything in it, after she'd breathed her last. But too bad to see it all go roaring up in flames . . . when you think about it."

Quietly and delicately, in someone else's voice, Waldo said, "Your point is well taken." There was something about his face, momentarily beaten, destroyed, that Celia wanted to look away from.

But why?—about a mere, now cumbersome possession, a contest with an unprincipled lout?

She held his champagne glass to him and aware of her eyes on his face he smiled a little and said into the telephone, "Perhaps I'm ready after all to have a little talk. I have some things to attend to—suppose you call back here at around four and we'll fix a place to meet. You'd hardly want to join us in our room because I might have the police waiting for you."

Bernard's voice was vastly pleased, and his words without his planning it cruel. "That's my good boy. That's my Waldo."

Waldo replaced the receiver so carefully that it frightened her a little.

"But what nonsense—surely it's just saber-rattling?" she said. "And if he's to be taken seriously, all you'd need would be a call to the Philadelphia fire department—or police—or both?"

"You have a touching faith in our guardians. Christmastime in a big city, the usual carnival of fires from tenement Christmas trees added to the everyday score."

He drained his champagne glass and refilled it. "Commissioner, would you mind having your men keep a twenty-four-hour watch on my house on Pine Street? My wife's cousin threatens to have some friends of his burn it down. And where are you calling from, Mr. St. Clair, about this house? Dublin. Are you a Philadelphia resident? No, New York. Why don't you come here and protect your own property if you really *believe*— No, that won't work, commissioner, because he says he's going to burn it down from Ireland, by telephone."

Waldo lit a cigarette. "And then we pause for a snort of laughter from the other end of the line."

"Then what exactly are we going to do now, about him?"

"A check won't work, he'll know we can put a stop on it, even if we could get our hands on any rich round sum immediately. I think"—he got up and went to the window, hands in his pockets—"maybe your idea is the best and the simplest. Let him have the house to sell and give him a commission, a little over and above what you'd pay an ordinary real estate outfit. With a written and witnessed agreement from him that this concludes the matter of his interest in the Gore house."

"But would a piece of paper stop him from pestering us all our lives? He got away with it once, why not a second time, and a third?"

"It's the immediate fire, excuse the expression, we have to put out," Waldo said. "We'll worry about the rest of it later. As Cy said, he'll be much easier to deal with at home, where he can be got at."

"Shall I come with you? After all, I'm the one who stuck you with him, and the house."

"No. Being Bernard, if he took my proposal amiss he might try to brain you with a beer mug or go for your throat the way he went for mine, with a little under fifty witnesses present." He looked at his watch. "I'm due shortly at the doctor's to have my head checked. It's a good thing he can't see inside it."

She got up to get dressed to go with him.

"No, don't, Celia. You'd better stay here for a bit, in case our friendly neighborhood bird dog calls—Cy. If we're both out he may think we're already entombed somewhere. After the doctor, I have a talented madwoman in Killeney, to see her Hibernian Hepworths, and then a stop at Leixlip, will you be all right?"

Only half-hearing, she said in the astonishment of returning to the ordinary, and the inescapable, "I have, God help me, shopping to do . . ."

He hadn't been gone five minutes before Cy called.

"Good morning, Celia darling. I want very much to see you but insane as it sounds when I'm planning to take you away from him with all possible speed, I didn't like to walk in on Waldo's birthday rites."

"But I thought you were leaving this morning, for Aberdeen."

Deliberately vague, he said, "There's been a hitch, it may be another day or so—" and sharply urgent, "What about Caldwell?"

She told him what about Caldwell.

He said in a puzzled way, "I suppose he knows what he's doing, meeting this man away from the hotel, I can only hope he's not going to spring another trap."

"He sounded," she said, surprised now at the recollection, "at first shattered, and as though he would faint, if men can, that is—"

"Shattered? The imperturbable Waldo? I've seen colossal sales slip through his hands, no fault of his, and he never bats an eyelash. What is this house anyway, the Taj Mahal of Pine Street?"

"No, only a big dark shabby brick house with a dirty front door and a broken shutter."

Shattered. Worrying the word like a bone, he asked on impulse, "What was her name, this aunt of yours?"

"The same as mine. Gore."

"Gore," he said prodding to himself. "Philadelphia . . . Gore . . ."

"Well, in any case, a few minutes later, after the call, he seemed calm, cool—and a little desperately on top of things. But for all I know that could be the effect of shock, the head wound—"

Cy wasn't entirely sure why he had deferred by telephone his meeting with a hard-up Scottish peer to discuss the purchase of his Reynolds.

A stitched and bandaged Waldo, a possibly imagined lethal attack on Celia, and Waldo's peculiarly blithe handling of these matters—"I will go and see him tomorrow and have what I hope will be a final interview" . . .

How did you have a decisive final interview with a walking, churning, unpredictable rage?

He remembered the violence in the gallery, the painting kicked brutally off the wall. "And if you think this is the end of it, it's just the beginning, Mr. Waldo your honor St. Clair."

He felt no reassuring certainty that, in her husband's care, bleak danger hovering, Celia could be considered safe.

CHAPTER 16

"What, speaking of the house, did you mean by all those jewels and other goodies that were to be kissed goodbye? I connected her somehow with paper napkins and canned milk."

Waldo was drinking whiskey with his attacker of the night before.

McGettigan's, shabby, dim, its air a stale haze of malt and tobacco, was in an alley off Sean McDermott Street near the canal. It was half a block away from Doreen's Banquet Street flat. When Waldo, during the telephone arrangements about a meeting place said, "It sounds like a dump," Bernard answered, "It happens to be convenient for me. I'm making the rules now, remember?"

In his usual rumpled state, he eyed Waldo when he came in at the swinging door with a combination of envy and disfavor. Dark turtleneck jersey, lithe black trousers, black raincoat carelessly open, dark blue knitted sailor's cap pulled down over his ears.

"You look either like a goddam ballet dancer or a cat burglar," he said.

"I had to start from the head down to cover up the bandage, and that pretty well dictated everything else. After we tidy up our affairs I'm going on to a birthday party."

And then, when his whiskey arrived, he asked his question about the house on Pine Street.

Bernard, bolstered with drink and power, was expansive. "I could spot the rings, big ones, under those crazy gloves of hers. And if she was so proud of that chair she gave me a peek at, she might have had other stuff like it. My mother told me long ago about a collection of silver—and then her old man, Laura's, was supposed to be rich as God, he built that house, there may be a lot of old out-of-date knickknacks . . ." Having excited himself with his guesses and hopes and fantasies, he said, "We may have a bloody goldmine on our hands!"

"Take it easy," Waldo said. "So far it's just a reasonably valuable piece of real estate sitting on a tough market, people aren't buying, it may be months, I'm told."

"I'm not prepared to wait months, or even weeks," Bernard said, signaling for another whiskey.

"So I gather." Waldo picked up his glass, took a drink, and studied his hand at close range. Perfectly steady.

He had rehearsed his script in the Mercedes, on the way to McGettigan's. The words came out just as he had intended them to do, bitten-off, unwilling and sullen.

"This burning business could be a bluff but you're"—he put a finger to the wound under the cap and the bandage—"not a man of what I'd call normal behavior. And then, Celia's thought all along that while you haven't a legal claim you have an unwritten one of sorts."

Should he chance another whiskey? Yes. He needed it.

"We're pretty well over the barrel financially speaking. Peanuts of course in the checking account, a few odds and ends tied up in mutual funds which have taken a hell of a beating—"

He knew Bernard would expect a wail about money.

The other man grinned. "You're making what the Irish call a poor mouth," he said. "As you said to me over the phone this morning, shove it. Don't tell me a man like you—your name over the door, your own business on Madison Avenue—can't raise money in an emergency."

"Then you won't see reason and wait till the house is sold?"

"No. Now. Or, you might say, now or never, there won't be any house to be sold."

Waldo sighed. "I spent summers here when I was in school, with a friend who is to say the least loaded. Dunfawny House, between Malahide and Swords. He breeds horses. I tried to

reach him a couple of times and finally did. But you can't borrow a large sum of money over the wires. At least not from him
you can't. I said I needed his help badly and all he asked was
how fast I could get there. He's off tomorrow to a horse auction in Donegal."

He was suddenly aware of the danger of seeming unlike himself, relaxed and cooperative. He came back visibly, for Bernard, from the pleasant cool green summers of his youth, the
horses and the woods and the meadows, the gray stone Georgian house mistily asleep in the sun or ghostly in the rain.

Voice crisp and harshly edged, he said, "With the wildest
kind of luck, I can probably get ten thousand from him. Dollars, that is, not pounds."

He watched the expressions chasing themselves over Bernard's face: triumph, greed, astonishment; then doubt in his
triumph, and another lick of greed.

Walking on eggs, as though the miraculous vision of actual
cash in hand would vanish, Bernard said, "Well, great to start
with. But that's nowhere near . . ."

Waldo waved an impatient hand. "After probate, you're to
handle the sale of the house. Ten percent of whatever it brings,
for you, you'll have a nice legal letter from us to that effect."

"Well now." Bernard beamed. "On that, Waldo, let's have
another drink."

"No, not another drink. You're driving us to Dunfawny
House. The car's just down the alley." He put his hand to his
head again and closed his eyes for a moment. "I thought a couple of times on the way here I was going to conk out, thanks to
you and your fist."

"Okay, fine," Bernard said. "I only hope I remember to stay
on the left. Put your money away. This is my treat."

They drove up the coast road, north; the same way the St.
Clairs had gone to Kelley Kelly's house.

Bernard was inclined to be propitiatory. He felt an iciness
and tension coming from Waldo, on the leather seat beside
him. Mind-changing at this point wouldn't suit at all.

". . . it must have been nice, when you were a kid, coming over here to stay. Horses and things. I always wanted to ride a horse . . . Westerns I suppose, clouds of dust, I liked the sounds of the hoofs . . ."

Waldo wanted no part of the proposed companionship and sharing of interests. He answered the stumbling confidence with contemptuous silence.

Doesn't like being the low man, Bernard thought. He's used to it way up there at the top. Giving orders, not taking them.

He felt a need to assert himself again. "How far away is this place? And what's the drill when we get there?"

"Ten more miles or so . . . you'll wait in the car for obvious reasons." Waldo took the last cigarette from his case and gave a short savage push to the dashboard lighter.

Uses it like a weapon, Bernard told himself, what if when it gets hot he holds it against my face or something?

He was a little frightened; the unfamiliar way of driving, the dark silent countryside, the taut stranger beside him. Triumph was leaking away along with the heat of rapidly consumed whiskey.

Hang in there, he exhorted. It's almost done. A nice fat certified check, a down payment that would clinch his ownership of his factory.

They descended the long hill where the Mercedes had been stopped on the grass verge a few nights before, and up another slope.

"Turn left here," Waldo said.

The headlights, as Bernard obediently swerved the wheel, caught an abandoned, broken white stucco farmhouse close to the road, its windows black and gaping, its thatched roof sagging.

"Left again."

"You're sure? It's nothing but a bloody lane."

"I'm sure."

Bernard put the car in second; this hill was almost as steep as the face of a cliff. At the bottom, there was a stream with a humped stone bridge over it and beyond the bridge another unused-looking building, very small, built of rough stones, windowless.

"Stop a minute," Waldo said. "I have to pee."

Not wanting, at this godforsaken end of nowhere to let his passenger out of his sight, Bernard said, "Good idea, me too."

He saw without thinking about it as he got out of the car Waldo reaching for the glove compartment and snapping it open. Flashlight, maybe. Or no, it must have been a fresh pack of cigarettes he was reaching for, he saw the glow from the lighter on Waldo's face.

Waldo walked behind the stone hut, turned around, waited a moment, listening, then walked back toward the car and when Bernard was six feet away from it shot him, at close range, three times, through the head.

The great shout of noise began receding into a gasping cry as the big heavy body plunged in slow motion forward, taking what seemed like forever to hit the ground.

Listen again. Listen with every pore of your body, not just your ears. Would the sound of the shots never stop re-echoing from the sheer hill behind them?

Headlights smote him, from the top of the hill. Bernard's body in its slow crash had efficiently hidden itself close along the car on the side away from the lane.

A cautious driver, taking the descent slowly, to judge from the headlights. Waldo stepped over the body and got into the car and moved behind the wheel.

The other car, a battered Ford Anglia, drew to a stop in the lane, beside the Mercedes.

A man's voice, soft, old, friendly, asked, "Are you in trouble then? Out of gas is it? I thought I heard backfiring—"

"No." Waldo put his head halfway out the window, willing the kind eyes to look at him, at this knitted cap and black-rimmed Woolworth glasses, and at nothing else. "Call of nature, just stopped for a minute, thanks anyway. I heard the backfiring too, ahead somewhere."

"Well, a very merry Christmas to you."

"And the same to you."

The Anglia moved leisurely forward, climbed the opposite hill and disappeared. The night was empty.

Waldo switched off the headlights and stole a few precious seconds to accustom his eyes to the darkness. He reached again into the glove compartment and got out a folded heavy plastic bag. He bent and with swift precision got the bag over Bernard's head and chest and secured it with nylon twine.

A great weight to drag, and the plastic was slippery, but the distance was short. Down a sloping soft earth path to the stone shepherd's hut. Deserted in the long-ago summers, deserted still, as he had verified during the day's various vital explorations. The door was half off its hinges.

He allowed himself the pencil illumination from a tiny pocket flashlight when he had pulled the door to again. The damp cold bit at him.

There was a trap door cut into the stone floor, with a heavy rusted iron ring at one end. He and Kevin, when they had stumbled on it in their wanderings, had thought it was probably a hiding place for illegally distilled poteen. The cavity under the floor was about eight feet deep and six feet long, with an iron ladder hanging against its wall.

A final push, a soft thudding crash, and then the gentle lowering of the stone slab. It was three inches thick and fitted tightly, cleanly back into place.

The pencil of light flicked the floor again. No blood, not a drop.

He examined the plaid wool muffler he had taken from Bernard's body and thrust into his raincoat pocket. Bloodless too.

There was blood on the gorse and grass beside the car but no doubt a helpful rainfall would soon dispense with it, wash away the last visible trace of Bernard Caldwell, deceased.

CHAPTER 17

Waldo had been gone for an hour and a half.

It seemed a long time for a simple business proposition but then Bernard wasn't a simple man, but a sort of human thunderstorm.

She occupied her restless hands in wrapping more presents bought earlier in the day, a bamboo-patterned silk robe, a leather flask of heathery cologne, a pocket computer; Waldo liked gadgets, played with them briefly, and then discreetly let them disappear.

How nice, how easy Christmas shopping had been when she was very young and very broke, she thought with a pang of nostalgia. Most of it done in half an hour at Woolworth's.

And you couldn't pay Waldo back with a heap of pretty packages, for not wanting to be his wife any more.

The ringing of the telephone sent a shock down her spine. It was Waldo, his voice peculiar.

"Christ, I've been waiting all this time and he hasn't shown up yet—has he called there by any chance?"

"No . . . hadn't you better come back?" Shd didn't like the sound of him at all; but then he was probably beside himself with raging impatience.

"I'll give him fifteen more minutes and myself one more drink. McGettigan's by the way is a pub we will not lift a holiday or anniversary glass in."

"I've ordered your birthday dinner, to be served up here about eight-thirty," Celia said, feeling as if it was someone else talking. "I didn't think you'd want to or should go out again."

The kitchen had been pleasantly cooperative, yes, indeed,

the gentleman's birthday—Waldo's favorite chicken breasts with mushrooms and artichoke hearts, in champagne sauce, an endive salad dressed with Roquefort whipped into wine vinegar, a small chocolate cake with a candle in the center. Waldo allowed himself cake once a year.

He laughed; again an odd sound, no merriment in it. "Birthday dinners in the middle of all this—all right, I won't be long. I suppose he won't put the place to the torch until he finishes trying to screw me blind. He probably ran into the open end of a bottle somewhere else . . ."

It was close to an hour before the door opened and he came in, breathless, as though he had been running.

Worried at his pallor, she said, "Well, did he finally—?"

"No, goddammit. I can only figure he got cold feet, thought I might be bringing the police with me—" He put both hands to his bare bandaged head.

Celia had at no time been interested in her bequest; now the house, the haunting house, seemed to her a grim burden, a menace, Laura Gore bent on sending misery along to them from the depths of the family mausoleum.

The house had pushed Bernard into the center of their existence, Bernard and his savage attack on the Green, and a just remotely possible shove in the back on Grafton Street.

Waiting for Waldo, she had been entirely with Cy; to make up for it, she gave him a surface tenderness and care, brought him aspirin, put a testing palm against his damp forehead, fixed him a drink and made one for herself. However many drinks he had consumed while waiting for Bernard, he seemed sober.

Drink wasn't what was wrong with him.

What *was* wrong with him? Besides an unkept appointment?

She lifted her glass. "Happy birthday again, Waldo."

"Happy *birthday!*" He got up and came over to her, pulled her to her feet and put his arms hard around her, burying his head against her neck.

"Celia . . . for my birthday present, I'm proposing marriage to you, our marriage. Will you be my wife, darling?"

In some way outraged, she tried to move away. His arms were like iron.

"Celia, please. I know about Cy, I know these things happen, but you haven't given either of us enough time to deal with it—"

She went very still against him.

Horrifyingly, he started to shake, his body beating like a drum.

"Darling . . . you can't, I need you . . . I feel lost . . . I feel like a kid alone in the dark . . . I'm *frightened* . . ."

If only he would stop shaking. Blithe Waldo, on top of things. Imperturbable, Cy had called him. Now, clutching her desperately, now at this moment a ruin.

She was totally unable to speak. He lifted his head and his eyes, near, burned into hers as they had when she woke to find him watching her in the silent early morning dark.

"Six months, please, Celia?" Please wasn't one of Waldo's usual words. "That isn't too long to ask, after five years . . . *please*. Jesus, I thought when I saw the empty bed before I came out here and found you that you'd packed up and gone off to him—"

In his present state and hers, she found it impossible to bring out an immediate flat refusal to his request. And was she trembling now, or was it merely her flesh picking up the rhythm of his? Her head felt as if it were going to burst.

"All right, Waldo—it has to be talked about, but—" She hardly knew what she was saying. Talked about? The fact that she was wholly, bone-deep, committed to another man? "All right, try to stop shaking, you scare me . . ."

Like a child, he put his knuckles into his eyes. She had never before seen him cry.

He turned his head sharply away. "Have another drink, Waldo, and come back to the human race," he said. "But first wash your face in cold water."

On his way back to his chair and his drink, he bent and lightly kissed her hair. She felt very cold and very empty. She managed a smile, got up with relief at the knocking on the door. Something, anything, to get over this encounter and its implications, echoing in her ears.

The dinner table was wheeled in with a flourish. A glistening array of covered dishes, lighted candles in crystal holders, a slender white vase of freesias and incredibly early white and yellow tulips.

They went through the motions, unfolded napkins, clinked glasses of pale golden chablis, determinedly lifted forks.

Waldo managed about half a chicken breast, got up abruptly, and went into the bathroom. She heard from behind the closed door the retching noises.

Yes, Great-aunt Laura, thank you very much for your house.

Cy, lonely in his big room at the Gresham, furnished it with Celia. Standing by the window, lamplight catching her shining hair. Pushing up her glasses into the brown shimmer when he bent his head to kiss her, and saying on a breath of laughter, "I hope I'll know who it is without my glasses, yes, I do, it's Cy isn't it, Cyril Francis Hall."

He had spent a restless afternoon prowling the National Gallery of Ireland, Dublin Castle, and streets and streets of the faintly sad finery of once grand Georgian houses still speaking in faraway voices of laces and satins, balls and smart uniforms, chandeliers blazing and music drifting through the great tall windows.

Now, unable to sit, to bury himself in his book or a newspaper, he stared at the telephone, willing it to do its job. Ring, produce information, reassurance, answer all the doubts, all the puzzles, all the questions.

There were a lot of them.

He felt a strong uneasiness about Celia, about the whole business, that wouldn't go away.

Why, really, were they here at all, so far from home, where Bernard could be dealt with?

He didn't fully believe in Waldo's attempt to save his marriage. Even when he had first heard it, it didn't sound right, it didn't sound like Waldo.

Passing Irena Tova's half-open door the day before he left for Paris, he had heard her soft possessive creamy voice, a dropped phrase or so . . . "Yes, Waldo darling, I am being beautifully good . . . well, yes, but it won't be long . . ." She didn't sound like a lover put firmly aside, given up as a bad habit. There was a sense of expectancy and lazy joy coming from her.

He neither liked nor disliked Waldo. His partner was passionately devoted to his work, a good and subtle salesman, an entertaining and amiable associate.

After all these years he was still somewhat of an unknown quantity. Gracefully self-assured, even a little secretive. Not a direct man; given to smiling plans, manipulations, as though following the adage that the longest way round is the shortest way home.

Shattered.

He kept coming back to the word. About a piece of real estate in Philadelphia?

He remembered Waldo saying to him, concerning the house, in answer to a casual polite inquiry, "Okay place, big, a bit shabby, and it may take months to sell. And then the capital gains tax . . . It's nothing to fire off Roman candles about."

The St. Clairs lived comfortably and as far as he was aware had no vast debts, heavy financial responsibilities and cares.

Celia was quietly accurate in her use of words, not given to overstatement. But this had been her spontaneous description of Waldo's reaction to the bizarre threat.

He remembered too, as his eyes prodded the phone, willing it to ring, that Celia had told him the sudden unwelcome decision to go away, to Ireland, had been presented to her the evening Waldo had come back from looking over her aunt's house.

And now the house was, in a sense, being held for ransom by the erratic violent cousin.

Could, for some reason or another possibly connected with Pine Street, Waldo be wanting to preserve his marriage, keep his wife at his side, for plain hardheaded financial reasons?

Nothing to do with vows, repentance, a fresh start—merely fasten her firmly to him again, hold on just as firmly to Irena, because from every worldly point of view it was more convenient for him, more practical.

It seemed to him to make greater sense than a sudden romantic turnabout.

Feeling that he was really getting nowhere, grappling at shadows, he ordered ice, poured scotch, and then for want of something more constructive to do went to the uncooperative telephone and put in a call to his friend John Van Loon in Philadelphia.

Van Loon, who didn't need the money but liked to have something to keep him occupied, owned a small elegant store on lower Pine Street in which he sold paintings and prints, antiques, and expensive greenery.

"Gore . . . Gore?" he mused in answer to Cy's inquiry. "Let me think. As a matter of fact, I'm right in the middle of selling an étagère, she's almost ripe and ready to spring for it . . . hang on a minute or so, you can afford it."

Coming back to the phone, he said, "Done! Now, Gore Back in my great-grandfather's day, he had a rich pal named Gore, Nathaniel I think, five or six houses, a yacht—I only remember the name because there's a family legend about heavy consumption of port while at sea, and great-grandpa fell overboard and almost drowned. Not at all the thing you like to connect with these Episcopalian ancients. Shall I look into it further?"

"Will you? There's a woman, dead, who may have been his daughter . . ." He gave Van Loon the details quickly, thinking of Celia perhaps needing him badly and getting a busy signal.

Silence. Perhaps by now a candlelit birthday dinner was in progress. This did not bear much thinking about.

He had another scotch, trying to gather the bits and pieces together. The house might be entirely irrelevant; he might be being swayed by the vagaries of his own business, relatives rousing themselves from their fresh grief wanting to know if Mother's collection of paintings might be valuable?

He himself had made discoveries, thrilling ones, in unlikely attics and closets. A rich pal named Gore, a clutch of houses, a yacht, and perhaps a daughter named Laura, an eccentric, a recluse, who drank tea with gloves on her hands for fear of dirt . . .

Underlining the house was Caldwell. His fanatical determination to pry loose a share of it, which had brought him across the Atlantic, a trip he could surely ill afford.

But, round and round. Why not stay in New York, Waldo, to run new riches through your fingers? The story about Mrs. Donahue's pressing desire for her Irish paintings hadn't been founded on fact.

Easy and obvious, that one: get her away from his partner Cy Hall while he tried to mend his fences, erase the hovering word divorce.

To hell with fastidious hanging back. He lifted the phone and dialed the St. Clairs' room.

Celia answered in a voice that could have been considered furtive until she explained just above a whisper that Waldo was sleeping, or trying to, in the bedroom.

"What happened, with Caldwell?" Cy demanded. "Has he been disposed of?"

"No." She murmured to him what Waldo had told her about his vigil at McGettigan's pub.

Very slowly, Cy said, "If I weren't unfortunately civilized, I'd say, come away with me, Celia, right now."

There was a silence. He thought he detected tears, recent or present, in the low voice. "I couldn't anyway, civilized or not . . . I promised Waldo another six months, to try to . . . he . . ."

Treacherous, impossible, to describe the brief awful crackup, even to Cy.

It was his turn for silence. Out of a cold rage, he said, "God you're easy to con. I hope your cousin doesn't get his hands on you."

He was immediately and bitterly sorry.

Six months could be dealt with, one way or another; she was for life, his life.

"To get back to the matter in hand, I don't understand it. He's pulled his ultimate threat, short of holding a gun at your head, or Waldo's. The prize is ready to drop into his hands. And then he doesn't show up."

He felt her trying to gather herself together. "Waldo thought at the last minute he might have been afraid he'd have the law with him."

"So there he still is, or there he still isn't," Cy said, trying to hold down another kind of anger. "What's your—marital decision now? Sit and wait with folded hands?"

Sounding as if, wearily, she didn't give a damn about what happened now, she said, "What else would you suggest, Cy?"

"I'll try to think of something. In the meantime"—this didn't seem a moment for endearments—"good night."

As, muscles almost aching with the sense of frustration, helplessness, he strode the room, his eye fell on the *Irish Times* flapped over a chair arm.

He picked it up, turned to the classified ads, found a number, and called it.

"I'm in a bit of a rush—I assume this will appear tomorrow morning? Good." And then he dictated: "For reasons of financial benefit to him, will Mr. Bernard Caldwell or anyone knowing of his whereabouts get in touch with Mr. C. H. at the Gresham." He gave his room telephone number and added, "Speed in this matter is of the utmost importance to Mr. Caldwell."

CHAPTER 18

Ordering breakfast, shaving, dressing, he waited for the sound of his chancy penny dropping: the telephone.

He thought Bernard Caldwell might be more willing to deal with a sort of neutral intermediary. Or might at least call him to investigate the alluring words "financial benefit" which few people can resist.

He could then explain to the shyly defaulting blackmailer the St. Clairs' offer to have him handle and profit by the sale of the house.

Breakfast was being wheeled in when the phone rang.

A woman's voice, Irish, a little breathless with apprehension or shyness.

"About your ad in the *Times* . . . I don't know if I'm doing the right thing but I came by anyway, I'm in the lobby—"

He put the greatest possible reassurance into his voice.

"Will you come right up? I'm just having breakfast." He gave her his room number and added, "Do you take tea or coffee?"

This hospitable afterthought seemed to disarm her. "Oh, tea, but I won't trouble you."

"No trouble at all." He ordered it and then stood at the half-open door so that she wouldn't feel any kind of trap was waiting to swallow her.

In his cream-colored corduroys and tattersall shirt, he looked to Doreen tall, worried, attractive, and for some reason entirely trustworthy.

She did give one instinctive raking glance about the room as if expecting to see a policeman pop up from behind the green and white striped sofa and then relaxed her clutch on the strap of her shoulder bag.

She refused to yield up her coat. "No, I dressed in such a hurry I'm any which way underneath . . . oh, here's my tea coming, aren't you nice."

She tried to lift the pot but her hand was shaking badly. He took it from her and poured tea and sat down across from her at the table, addressing himself to his bacon and eggs.

"I'm that upset," she explained, about her shakes. "It's just that I couldn't sleep, I was so worried about him."

She managed a sip of the tea and straightened her back. "I suppose if I had a brain in my head I would have asked before I came up here who you are and what you want with him, he'd probably kill me if he caught me meddling in his private affairs, but—"

Cy identified himself, and seeing no reason for shadow-boxing with this tired-eyed woman whose presence somehow suggested a comfortably rumpled bed, good food, and a bright fire, went on, "I'm Waldo St. Clair's partner. He has a proposition to put to Caldwell, all fair and square, and can't seem to be able to make contact with him."

"I don't follow that, I don't follow that at all. It was he, the St. Clair fellow, that Bernie went to meet."

"Yes, but it never came off."

"Then why did he tell me he was meeting him? We're just"—she blushed—"friends for a short time, but he's been very open with me about his problems, his family troubles."

"Have you any idea where they were supposed to meet?" He drank coffee and refilled her cup.

"No, but I thought it would be near where I—" She bit this off. "I mean, he doesn't like to spend money on taxis and he doesn't know his way around the bus routes yet. After an hour went by, and then another— I had a nice piece of beef for him and he said he hadn't had roast potatoes since he was a kid, peeled, you know, and browned in the fat—"

She stopped and stared ahead of her. Remembering what country he was in, Cy got up, took a bottle of scotch from the chest of drawers, and said, "A drop in your tea?"

"Oh, I couldn't, unless you . . ."

"Of course I am."

He poured a generous dollop into her strong dark tea and an equal portion into his coffee. She downed hers in two grateful gulps and fresh, country pink came into her cheeks.

She said mistily, "When I think of the poor fellow, all those years, the faithful visits of him, sitting at her feet, taking her lip, given to understand he'd have his fair share . . ." With the characteristic Irish way of improving and embellishing a story, she went on, "God knows there's plenty to go round, not counting the property. All those pearls and diamonds, and paintings and silver and grand furniture, it's a sin what they get for old stuff in the antique shops. The place is a regular mint."

Allowing for exaggeration, his, the big-talking American salesman, and hers, he filed this away.

"And no word from him whatever last night, no call, nothing?"

"No. He'd had a little . . . unpleasantness with Mr. St. Clair the night before and I thought maybe he'd run into trouble so after the two hours I went looking in the pubs for him. The thing is that when you describe him he sounds like other people."

"Nobody could say for sure they did see him?"

"There's a place called McGettigan's where he might have been. Or someone like him."

"Was he with anybody?"

"Yes, for a little while." Indignantly she said, "The bartender'd had a skinful himself. All I could get out of him was that the other fellow had on some kind of knitted seaman's hat. And, oh yes, big black-rimmed glasses."

"Have you gone to the police to report him missing?"

She gave him a horrified look. "I wouldn't want to meddle to that extent. Maybe he just . . ."

The thought hung unsaid between them. Maybe he had abruptly tired of her, and walked out, and away, for good.

Cy put his next inquiry very delicately.

"Seeing he was expecting to come back to you for dinner, did he by any chance leave anything at your place?"

She seized at this face-saver. "Yes. A small case, and his old raincoat, he'd bought a new one."

"What was he—"

Peculiar slip on his part, he thought.

"What is Caldwell like? If I'm to act as a go-between, it would be helpful to know."

She was caught in an obvious struggle between her loyalty to Bernard and her liking for this amiable, tea-providing, whiskey-pouring stranger, this mysterious but comforting ally.

"Big, a bit rough around the edges, wants taking care of," she said confidingly. "Bit of a temper, apt to flare up, I'd put it down to being neglected or abused when he was a kid. Not that he's turned it on me yet. He likes his own way and doesn't take kindly to interference."

Pressed by a sense of urgency he couldn't define, he said, "You'll let me know if you hear from him later in the day? You have my number."

"Yes. After all"—she looked wistful, and lost, and then hopeful again—"tomorrow's Christmas."

"And may I have your number? Just in case—"

She gave it to him after a moment of holding back. He had an idea that on her own she was an open woman, but that Bernard had pulled her into his plots and plans, his secrets and silences, and caused this behavior change.

"Just one more thing," he said as she stood up to go. "If you don't hear so much as a whisper from him"—my God, he thought, I'm talking Irish already—"you might be wise to take a look through his—whatever it was he left with you. Not to snoop, but to see if there are things he must have, and that no matter what, he'd come back to you for. That way, you'd know whether it was worth worrying about or not, he may just have run headfirst into a party or something—"

He let her fill it in for herself, the bleary awakening, the confused recollection, sometime late in the morning; the dash for the phone or the expensive taxi.

"A good idea. I will. Am I to put the proposition to him?"

"No. I want to do that myself."

"All right then, and thank you for the tea." She left with an air of renewed optimism: in one way or another, she had managed to put Bernard back, for herself, into the present tense.

Late in the morning, Cy called John Van Loon in Philadelphia.

"Did I get you up?"

"No, I'm an early riser, just finished breakfast. The ancient Gore daughter *was* named Laura, if that's any help."

"I hate to bother you further, but is there any way you could get yourself into her house and take a look around? It's a long story and I won't bore you with the whys and wherefores. Could you be, say, a friend of the St. Clairs requested to give a rough evaluation of the furnishings for them, you being the expert?"

"I don't know why not, I love to eavesdrop on other people's houses. I'll find out if there's a caretaker in residence or if not I'll track down who it is, what firm, that handles the Gore affairs and present myself to them. I am, after all, a perfectly respectable Pine Street crook. It may take a day or so, Christmas tomorrow—I'm having a nonstop Christmas Eve punch party at the store."

"Couldn't you slip out between drinks?" Cy looked at his hand on the receiver and felt the cold dampness against the plastic.

Why? Just thoroughness, this, finding the answers to mild puzzles. Why the sense of something picking up a kind of terrifying speed?

"All right. But don't hold your breath until I call back. If for any reason I can't make it, or can't get in, Merry Christmas."

Mildly inebriated but grown increasingly curious during the day, he visited the Pine Street house in an appropriate thick snowfall a little after six o'clock. He had called first and been answered by an old, cautious black voice.

"I'm sorry," she said to his request, on the phone. "I've been told there's to be no one allowed into this house."

"Waldo called me today from Ireland, Mr. St. Clair that is. He must be pretty anxious about it to spend all that money."

At the enormity of a long-distance call all the way across the ocean, she capitulated.

But she followed four or five feet behind him as, after entering the house, he began lifting the ticking covers, with an occasional sneeze.

Standing in the hall, his hand caressing a lacquered surface, he said softly, "Jesus Christ."

Censoriously, she heard him, two more times, take the name of the Lord in vain.

After that, poking and prowling, room after room, floor above floor, he seemed to find nothing whatever to say.

Doreen had two massage appointments during the morning and was grateful for them, take her mind off her troubles, all that hard work.

She got back to her flat in Banquet Street a little after one o'clock and made a pot of tea for refreshment and courage.

Then, guiltily, she approached the suitcase, left trustingly with its lid slightly open on the floor beside the bed.

His other suit, the blue. Dirty socks which she'd wash out later. A paperback with a nude on the cover, which she immediately and modestly looked away from; the title was *The Busy Body*. A permanent-press white shirt, also in need of washing. Plaid wool robe and slippers. A jar of instant coffee, helpful when you couldn't afford room service. Two ties, a half-full carton of cigarettes, startlingly bright magenta underpants.

In the shirred pocket on the underside of the lid, she found his checkbook, his passport, and a little black folder of American Express traveler's checks in fifty-dollar denominations, which flipped through came to four hundred and fifty dollars.

Didn't want to carry them around with him, she supposed; he'd told her that Christmas was a terrible time for pickpockets, in the States.

Oh then, he'll be back, Doreen told herself. She felt warmed and comforted. A man might, in a mood, leave a woman behind him. But never his passport and his money.

CHAPTER 19

Caught up in an almost febrile gaiety—a little above and beyond normal, at a pitch she found impossible to match—Waldo tried to provide her with a festive Christmas Eve.

"No more shopping, no more presents, you've given me you."

And, "Now that I've got you back I don't want you away from my side . . ."

He took her to his favorite pub, Lacey's on the Liffey. "I practiced Guinnessing here when I was a kid, with several immersions along the way." They drank lager and ate sandwiches of cheese and chutney, and after this homely meal he said, "Just to clean our teeth, my special peppermint."

This was a drink he had invented, copious shots of white crème de menthe in champagne. He liked to sip it, back at home, in the morning, after a late partying night.

The bartender made a face at himself with the mirror as he mixed the drink. Personal peculiarities were a way of life in his country, but to put the kiss of death on an expensive bottle of Piper Heidsieck—!

Ducking down behind the bar, he took a small sip and liked it. Afterward, the odd brew was added to Lacey's repertoire. Champagne St. Clair, it was called.

People, sampling it, thought with an edge of pleasure that the drink was named after something horrible that had happened; but they couldn't recall quite what.

Musing sadly that things brought to them in glasses, no matter how exotic, would not cure whatever was wrong with the two of them, Celia said, lovely, but they must save some of their strength for evening cocktails and dinner.

"The hell with that, eat, drink, and be merry," Waldo said. He put his hand on hers. "It would be a little merrier if you would stop looking as if you'd lost your last friend."

Lifting the minty champagne, Celia clinked glasses and said, "Speaking of being merry, do you know what we're going to do tomorrow . . . Christmas? What with minor disasters, I haven't made any coherent plans. Have you?"

She tried to do something about her face, her manner, her look of loss. It hadn't quite hit her yet, fully, but there was a cold and growing loneliness wrapping itself around her.

Six months, half a year, and possibly, probably, all of a life. Hers. Plenty of time for Cy to readjust his sights.

Celia mentally wrote a script for him. My nice shortsighted girl in her glasses, there's something about her, or about the two of us when combined, but why break up a marriage people are working at? Why all the thunder and lightning when things, rearranged, can be safe and simple and sweet.

From a humming distance, Waldo was saying, ". . . a duty, and I hate to leave you alone, but you'll be doing *your* duty, on your knees at mass."

She had, she saw, completely lost the first part of what he had been telling her, about Christmas Day.

It wouldn't do at all to say, sorry, I have no idea of what you've been talking about.

To cover this lapse, she asked with assumed concern, "But what about him—Bernard—waving his lighted match? He might just tell his Philadelphia worthies to go ahead with their kerosene cans."

"Not until he gets a counteroffer. It may be our face but it's his nose he's cutting off, if you get me." He glanced at his watch. "And you may not have noticed I've developed a new tic, checking for messages on the hour. It's about time to call again now."

When they left Lacey's they saw the tinker woman coming toward them along the sidewalk, her gait somewhat rolling. She stopped beside them. In spite of drink, broken teeth, and tangled red hair, there was something strangely handsome about her, jaunty, indestructible. The child on her hip was softly crying.

"Go ahead, celebrate," she said to Celia. "You haven't much time for it. Enjoy your last birthday of Christ."

Waldo, looking into the flashing eyes, said, "For a present to my wife, I'll buy off your curse." He took out his billfold and gave her a pound note.

She took it in one swift whipping gesture, pocketed it, touched his cheek with dirty fingers and said, "I think it's too late now, lovey, but then you never know, do you," and walked swiftly on before the donation could be withdrawn.

That's the third time, Celia thought. Three times unlucky. She was not superstitious as a rule. Her only concession to dark mysteries was an occasional knock on wood when she made a confident statement such as, that it had been a year since she'd had a cold.

But the tinker woman put her in mind of ancient tribal curses, rites, that preconditioned the victim to his death, perhaps made him unconsciously look for it, fatally removed the instinct for and belief in survival, the tiny and all-important flame blown out.

"God, Celia, you look green," Waldo said. "You don't believe in her blatherings, do you?" He hailed a cab. "There's something in a shop on Dawson Street I want you to have but you must try it on first."

"Oh, Waldo, you already have such a stack of things for me—" She felt wearily disinclined for trying on garments, but he insisted.

It was a long dress of misty gray chiffon, at once demure and sexy, with a cape-veil of chiffon floating over her arms and drifting to the hem at the back; it cost a ridiculous amount of money but Waldo said she must have it, she looked marvelous in it.

From somewhere, she summoned up enthusiasm, gratitude. "Yes, it's very pretty, even though"—with an uneasy picture of the red-haired woman, *your last birthday of Christ*—"it looks a little like a high-class shroud . . . thank you, Waldo."

Passing a small white Catholic church, she said impulsively, "Will you wait a few minutes for me? I want to go in and un-curse myself."

Shadows and silence, candles flickering, a few bent shawled heads; three children kneeling wide-eyed in front of the crèche beside the altar. She went and knelt beside them.

She prayed for herself, and for Waldo, and a little guiltily for Cy. It had taken her a great many years to see that prayer was not so much a matter of asking for something as a clear state-ment of what was really important to you; a definition of who you were, and what you lacked, what you were sorry for, what you wished to be. A peeling away to your essence.

"I'll try, with Waldo," she said mentally, to God or herself. "I will, I will."

With a Waldo she had never known: inexplicably, briefly, wrecked.

A little girl beside her looked away from her face in embar-rassment. A great grownup lady gazing at the straw and the lit-tle painted porcelain figures and animals and the dusty blue velvet backcloth with tarnished sequins on it for stars, tears coming out from under her glasses and rolling down her cheeks.

They stopped at the doctor's for Waldo to get his bandage changed. He came out of the consulting room with a neat and narrow one around his head, dramatically emphasizing his skin and hair.

There was no message from Bernard at the hotel desk but a Katherine Croix desired Waldo to call her. His face bright-ened. "Very festive sort of woman," he told Celia. "An Ameri-can, married Irish whiskey money here."

Festivity was indeed her idea. When, upstairs, he called her she said, "This is frightfully last-minute, darling, but I didn't know until lunch today with Cy that you were in town." And would they please, please, if they had no other plans, come to her Christmas Eve party, and help decorate the tree and light the candles? "In this holy land, on this holy-day, Dublin dims down," Katherine Croix explained. "You have to turn to a rank Protestant for a little uninhibited glee. And do dress up."

Waldo said they would love to come.

Rain mixed with snow came along with the early dark. They worked, each in their own separate ways, at trying to nap. They shared a late tea, with crumpets all but simmering in fragrant butter, and tiny chocolate éclairs. As usual before parties, Waldo counseled her to line her stomach well, and then she could let things rip. He showered, and she bathed.

"Wear your new dress, Celia." He was intent in the pier glass on his black tie. He went to the closet. "Do you suppose the butler will let me in without dancing pumps?"

He picked up a pair of fine narrow black calf shoes he had bought in London, in St. James's Street, and shoehorned them on.

Lamplight gleamed on the toes of the shoes. Celia stared at one of them, transported out of the warm flowery room into a chaos of remembered terror and darkness, and a splash of bouncing rain on her cheek.

The smack of the body against hers, the backward fall, her head striking the pavement, and a few inches away from her eyes and spotlit with gold from a shop window, an elegant black leather toe with a tiny scratch up the center of it. Forgotten until now, dredged up only because Waldo's right shoe had a tiny scratch in the same place.

Shock tingled in her fingertips.

Two absolutely opposed trains of thought presented themselves simultaneously.

One was—the merest glimpse of a dark bird in flight seen out of the corner of the eye—If it was Waldo who tried to shove me under a bus, of course he'd stand still for a few seconds, innocent onlooker, one of a crowd, it wouldn't do to cut and run guiltily and be described as doing so to the police, after they gathered up the extinguished body.

The other was, Thinking like this must be some mad revenge

on him because he wanted me, he got me, back. Destroyed and shaking . . . don't leave me, I feel like a kid in the dark . . . Invent insane persecution, make him a murderer, just because with a certain desperation he had retrieved his wife—

Then one huge simple fact broomed through her racing mind.

Waldo had no earthly reason to kill her.

"Why are you staring at my feet?" he asked. Her wild speculations had occupied only a flick of time.

Common sense lay within immediate reach. She took a firm hold on it.

"Was I . . . ? You've got a scratch on one toe."

"I hadn't noticed. Cold cream to the rescue. In the medicine cabinet?"

"No . . . let me look." She found a slim plastic bottle of Eve of Roma Cleansing Emulsion and watched him as, shoe on the edge of the tub, he fingered cream into the scratch and buffed it with a paper tissue.

Graceful and gleaming, black and white, he looked at her standing in the door of the bathroom.

He said, "It wouldn't do at all to be askew and disheveled when you and I walk into a party and come face to face with the late—for both of us—Cy Hall."

CHAPTER 20

Unable to put it away, she asked unwillingly in the taxi, "What do you mean, the late Cy Hall?"

"Oh, come," Waldo said, his voice still a little higher than normal, a suppressed excitement behind it. "You've agreed that at least for the time he's over for you, and can you see me rubbing elbows every day and drinking morning coffee with my wife's enraged ex-lover?"

There was an odd glow on his face, a deep sparkle in his dark eyes.

"Anyway, I've had it as a second-class citizen. Errand boy. Purveyor of the pop slop at Hall and St. Clair. So it couldn't be a better time to have him buy me out, I've had my eye on a gallery that *I* could be Cy Hall in. Now that his chapter has more or less closed."

Her own voice was strange to her too, remote. How final he made it sound, how very over. "Where"—not that she at all cared—"will you get the money?"

"The word among married couples, in case you'd forgotten, is 'we.' And you seem also to have forgotten that we have certain assets now."

"If they survive," Celia said and, chilled, drew herself deeper into her corner of the cab.

Cy was late at Katherine Croix's.

He said to himself that, with every sympathy for Doreen McGrath, he didn't want to leave any Bernard unturned. She hadn't called him with a report, cheerful or otherwise. He had called her twice but had only his own ring to listen to.

No one else had answered his classified ad.

He directed his cab to her address, found in the telephone book.

"Banquet Street is it?" the driver asked, looking over his shoulder at his passenger's immaculate dinner clothing. "First time to my knowledge pair of black trousers with satin stripes down the sides ever made their way into that particular thoroughfare."

Turning a corner from Doan Alley into Banquet Street, Cy saw illumined by a streetlight a shabby gold-lettered sign over a window. "O'Cummins and Sons. Wills. Conveyancing."

Wills. ". . . he might have had some wild idea that it would come to him as next of kin . . . not knowing I'd willed everything I died possessed of to Waldo . . ."

He didn't know where the thought had come from, or why, and dismissed it with dislike.

"Here's the grand ballroom you're after wanting." The driver stopped before a smoke-stained brick house in a row of its duplicates, with a peeling blue front door.

Probably a waste of time, but there was the possibility that Doreen had gotten her man back and now wanted no part of the inquisitive Mr. C. H. of the Gresham Hotel; or had been ordered by Bernard to drop the matter.

He knocked crisply and listened for furtive hushing noises, people staying still, waiting out the knocking. Instead, the door was flung wide and he saw with regret the pour of color, hope, dying away again from the woman's white skin.

"Come in, Mr. Hall," she said on a recovered breath, eyeing his penguin black-and-white. "My room isn't dressed for you but you're more than welcome."

Her look at the door had been all the answer he needed but he followed her in anyway. Small shabby living room comforted by a fire, doors confidingly open, showing a kitchen with a gas stove so old its metal legs were Queen Anne-shaped, another door open into a bathroom.

Apologetically, wiping her soapy hands on her apron, she said, "I was just washing out his socks and shirt."

Establishing for herself, Cy thought, a homely kind of continuity.

"Not a word from him? From anyone?"

"Not a word. Of course I was out this afternoon, working, but he had his key—" She caught herself. "Will you have whiskey?"

"Thank you, but I'm on my way somewhere."

"Somewhere can wait another ten minutes." He saw that this company reassured her; stranger that he was, he was someone she could talk to, about this peculiar frightening darkness that had fallen upon her. She poured Thomas Powers generously into two glasses and went for a pitcher of water.

The telephone rang and she darted for it. Her shoulders instantly drooped. ". . . and to you, too, a very happy one. No, I'm not spending the day at my sister's this year, I'm expecting a friend, an American friend . . ."

She took a drink of her Thomas Powers and, sitting in a rocker across from Cy, said, "I thought, many's the time today, of calling that St. Clair man, to see if he'd managed to arrange his meeting. Somewhere. But I hadn't the nerve. I could just hear him saying, And who are you, and what is your association with Mr. Caldwell?" She emptied her glass and looking into it added, "I thought, God bless him, Bernie maybe wouldn't want him to know about me . . . it's just been a few days, but still—"

She flicked a finger under one eye and then the other, catching up the drops.

"And you still don't want to go to the police?"

"No. Have them hunting him down like a beast just because I don't know where he is? After all"—she looked at his suitcase, visible through the door, beside the bed—"his things are here, I took your hint and went through them—his money and passport." As if the suitcase was a talisman, a firm promise of its owner's return.

Then she said, as much to herself as to him, "And tomorrow's Christmas. People want some kind of, I don't know, company, festivity, they don't like to be alone. I think, don't you? that"—on a long sigh—"tomorrow one way or another should decide everything."

"Charming couple. Just married, are they?"

The speakers were two of the forty-six guests at the Croixs' tree-trimming party. The tree stood thirteen feet tall in green magnificence in one corner of the long drawing room, missing the airily plaster-garlanded ceiling by only another foot.

Celia was at Waldo's prodding wearing her hated contact lenses. As usual, they irritated and burned her eyes and it was an effort not to keep idiotically blinking.

She looked softly ghostlike in her gray chiffon, and, for a nice-looking girl, oddly beautiful, someone fresh out of a legend.

Waldo, normally a cool and circumspect husband in front of other people, was giving her the attentions of a lover. He too looked at his best, his color high, under the olive skin, his snowy bandage a startling decoration around his head.

He had made Katherine Croix giggle, explaining the bandage in a perfectly straight-faced manner. "A distant cousin of Celia's knocked me out in Stephen's Green and on the way to the ground I hit a tree. Is that caviar I see over there?"

She was a tiny woman, pale, with immense pale lavender-blue eyes and improbable but real black eyelashes. She said, "Your Celia looks ravishing," and then without any intention of connecting two thoughts, "Cy ought to be on his way, isn't this a grand reunion?"

"Grand indeed," Waldo said lightly. "I can't seem to shake him. Three thousand miles, and he's stepping on my heels. Speak of the devil. Good evening, Cy."

Celia was on her knees beside the tree, fastening on ornaments so old and frail and lovely that she was almost afraid to touch them. Xavier Croix was high on a ladder above her; she was one of a laughing, chattering circle beneath. Waldo went over to her, put an arm about her waist and tenderly lifted her to her feet.

Startled, she turned and saw Cy, an unreadable expression on his quiet face. Or was it that he was looking quizzical.

"Darling, say hello to my partner. You remember Cy Hall?" The voice going up that one strange note again, Waldo above himself. His arm was still around her waist.

With Waldo watching her face from a few inches away, she hardly dared look at Cy, but instead comprehended him through every nerve end.

She felt the warmth flooding the skin of her face, uncomfortable, betraying.

". . . *do you always go around with all twelve wicks of your candelabra lit up?*"

Waldo dropped his arm and said to Cy, "Can we retire to the conservatory or somewhere? I have a bone to pick with you, and then we'll all be merry together. Back to your angels and cornucopias, Celia," giving her her directions to stay out of this in an amiable husbandly manner.

In the great vaulted glass-roofed room, breathing damp and the scent of tuberoses and lilies, and inhabited only by one other man, elderly, going about putting his nose into flowers, he said, not in his party voice, "What the hell do you mean by putting an ad in the *Times?* 'For reasons of financial benefit to him, will Mr. Bernard Caldwell—For Christ's sake what business is this of yours?"

"And here I thought I was doing you a favor," Cy said blandly. "It occurred to me that—to paraphrase the hair coloring people—with Caldwell, the closer you come the worse you look, to him. God knows *I'd* hate to have you as an adversary, Waldo. Whereas he has nothing to fear from me, an interested bystander. Very interested."

"Will you, beginning now, keep your hands not only off my wife but out of my private business?" He was trying to keep his voice low but savagery raised it a little. The flower-sniffing man regarded him with mild curiosity and thought it would be too bad if a fight broke out here between them, pots might go crashing—

Falling into the idiom of the country, Cy said, "That's as may be," and turned and walked calmly away.

Waldo's white patches showed again, for a flickering second.

The music started at eleven, the musicians gathered about the grand piano, violin, saxophone, trumpet.

The chandelier and lamps had been dimmed, candles lit on the great glistening tree and in the tall windows. People moved a little dreamily to the music.

Waldo was dancing with his hostess when a hand reached down to Celia, sitting on the sofa beside a talkative witty columnist from the *Irish Times*.

Cy took her socially and allowably into his arms. They had never danced together before.

A little out of control of herself, she melted to him without knowing she was doing it.

He looked down into her eyes and said prosaically and endearingly, "You said those things hurt you, to wear."

"They do, a little, but Waldo wanted me at my best for this particular scene . . ."

"Well, it worked, you're at your best. For Waldo."

Watching them go by, the man said to his wife, "I thought you said she was just married? But to the other one, the dark one . . ."

She gave the pair a considering look and shrugged. "Oh well . . . Americans . . ."

Looking over Cy's shoulder at the magical tree, a towering monument to the loss of early wonder, laughter, gaiety, Celia said, "Well, Merry Christmas, Cy, if we don't see you again . . ."

"You probably won't. But now that I've been laundered like

a batch of currency, I'll feel free to call you and say goodbye—
to you and Waldo."

When he got back to the Gresham, there was a message to
call John Van Loon.

He listened to the voice stammering with excitement, rummaging for adjectives. Fabulous. Incredible. Unbelievable. And
was there any chance that he might slither in before the auction and wander about, see all those glories by daylight—not
that he could afford—

Cy said he'd have to talk to the owners about that, thanked
him for his trouble, and added holiday wishes.

Undressing, he thought this offered a perfectly clear explanation of why Waldo, as well as wanting to keep his love, wanted
to keep his wife.

Of course he did.

He found himself wrestling with something he didn't understand except perhaps in a far dark impossible glimmering.

They were all momentarily caught like flies in amber,
Doreen forever waiting, Bernard eternally expected to return
for his passport and his traveler's checks, and his freshly laundered shirt and socks. Waldo drifting back in time, in an
impassioned courtship of his wife. And Celia, with violence
hanging . . . a fist, or a knife, or a shove.

Perhaps Mr. C. H. and his classified ad had been a mistake,
although his intentions had been of the best; perhaps he had
been one too many for the erratic cousin. Doreen, in spite of
her look of acceptance, of honesty, could have warned him off.
Stopped some clock.

The clock had to be started again; it was unnerving, infuriating, not to know what time of your life, and Celia's, it was.

It might be wise to remove the extraneous man from the
Gresham, get rid of the helpful go-between C. H., and let Bernard emerge breathing freely from his hole, listen to sense and
money talking, and go away, go home, to his bowling alleys and
Ping-Pong balls.

He reached for the telephone directory and called the Russell. Nothing, sorry, sir. The Royal Hibernian was severely pressed but came up with a five-room suite, which he engaged to take the following morning.

As far as they all knew, he would be gone, and they could start their clock ticking again, tidily dispose of their piece of business.

Without even looking squarely at it, he thrust the other, insane, reason for his expensive disappearance aside.

CHAPTER 21

Seeing Cy's tall, straight, retreating back going down the Croixs' grand stairway—as from a small tossed boat watching the reassuring cliffs draw away—Celia applied herself to champagne.

The result of this determined and useless celebration was that she woke with a head like a floating kite Christmas morning, to study with astonishment Waldo dressing in the midnight darkness. He was showered and shaved, and his vigorous purposeful motions rebuked the confusion of her brain.

Lashes concealingly lowered, she watched him pull on his knee socks, button his shirt, zip his trousers, consider a choice of shoes and settle on the black moccasins, pull out a striped tie and swiftly knot it.

Time to try her voice; just as she'd feared, husky, dry-throated. "Waldo . . . where on earth are you going at this hour?"

With exaggerated patience, he said, "I told you yesterday, when you were so busy not listening to me . . ."

"Well, tell me again."

"Sorry to sound bitchy." He came over and bent down and kissed her. "Merry merry, darling."

Beyond his head she saw the gaily stacked presents on the dresser which must have been arranged by him after she'd gone off to sleep. And where had the two immense potted poinsettias, flanking the arrangement, come from?

Enjoy your last birthday of Christ, the tinker woman's voice exhorted her. You only thought of ridiculous things like that because it was so very dark outside, and perhaps because of champagne haunting you.

There was a knock at the sitting room door and a waiter came in with a tray, breakfast for one.

"I didn't think you'd want yours at this ungodly hour," Waldo said. "It's barely seven."

Sitting in the tulip-printed chair by the window, he drank his coffee and ate his toast—no trencherman's breakfast this morning—and told her he was going to pay a duty Christmas visit to Kevin Royce's aunt at Dunfawny House.

". . . I thought you'd had your fill of ailing old ladies. She's just, at seventy, lost her sight and I'm not sure anyway she'd be up to a stranger under the circumstances. But she was very kind to me, all those summers . . ."

He would not, he said, take the car. There was a good fast train; Kevin would pick him up at the station. He fingered his bandage thoughtfully. "I hope the X-rays were right, I never know when a Bernard headache is going to descend on me, and it does something peculiar to my eyes."

He poured another cup of coffee and brought it to her. "We'll have our own celebration when I get back. You're to open absolutely nothing. I'd suggest, for the hangover you're so bravely concealing, a lot more sleep and then of course you'll be at church—I shouldn't be back later than early afternoon. What mass are you going to, in case I have to call you about the train back?"

"Nine . . . you ought to know that I'm in no state for solemn high."

Normally, when she went off to church, Waldo would bid her in the indulgent manner of nonbelievers, "Say a prayer for me." As though if it couldn't help it couldn't hurt either. He omitted this directive as he bent to kiss her goodbye.

"Don't forget to check the desk for messages. And I suppose before I go"—his hand hovering over the bedside telephone—"it would be only politic to wish Cy a good journey. In case I change my mind about Hall and St. Clair. We had what is known as words, last night, about you."

He called the desk at the Gresham. Celia heard the crisply delivered information: "Sorry, sir, Mr. Hall checked out not ten minutes ago."

"So that's that," Celia said brightly, wretchedness taking her like a tide.

On her way out to mass, she was signaled by the desk. "Note for you, Mrs. St. Clair, just left."

A plain cheap white envelope with her name typed on it and down in one corner, B. Caldwell.

"Who brought it?"

"I don't know, I've come on this minute myself, Daisy handed it to me, we were going to send it up."

She put it between the pages of her missal with an odd feeling that it would be safer and more comfortable to read it in church.

There were no elegant midnight mass people at St. Margaret's this morning, but mostly old men, old women, and children.

Whoever ran the church was having no part of the colloquial mass; it started and continued richly and solemnly in Latin.

During the Confiteor, she read the note. "Dear Celia, I'm sorry to say I don't trust your husband but that's a fact, to meet him, I mean, I thought he'd be likely to think up some kind of smartass trap." X-ings out, strikeovers, fingers ineptly picking at what looked, from the typeface, to be an antiquated machine. "Right from the beginning you seemed to see my side of it. I'll deal with you but not with him. Let's you and I talk about whatever he was going to offer, right away. I have a standby reservation on an afternoon plane, I'm pretty well flat out of money. I don't want to put a foot into Dublin for reasons stated—a friend I met in a pub is putting me up in his place here, he's a sort of gatekeeper and poacher-chaser and gardener. It's not far from where you are, between Dun Laoghaire and Dalkey a bit up from the bay, see map at bottom. I'm trusting in you and counting on you not to bring him with you, if he turns up I swear to God I'll pick up the phone and do what I said I was going to do."

Clever of him, unexpectedly so, she thought; nothing incriminating on paper, but the meaning was explicit.

"Gloria in excelsis Deo," intoned the priest triumphantly, "et in terra pax homibus bonae voluntatis . . ."

". . . I'm sure you'll be glad to see an end to this and I know I will. Hoping to see you this A.M. and wrap it all up with a friendly drink. Sincerely, B. C." The initials in heavy smeared black pencil.

She thought it over as clearly as she could during mass.

He had shown himself to be a dangerous man; but other voices in her head provided eager answers to that. Why on earth should he harm her, coming to him with a clear-cut business offer, he with a reservation, a plane to catch?

And what a marvelous Christmas present to Waldo, to her, getting finally rid of him; he had been in a way her responsibility all along.

A third, smaller voice told her that perhaps the recklessly accepting, don't-give-a-damn energy that rose in her could be champagne, sneakily lingering in her bloodstream; or might derive from the recollection of the desk clerk's crisp voice, "Mr. Hall checked out not ten minutes ago."

Hardly able to sit, to kneel, she left St. Margaret's right after communion, to disapproving stares from the congregation.

Standing on the steps, waiting for her, was Cy.

"Here, don't faint," he said, alarmed, taking her hand. "I called the Shelbourne, they said they thought you were off to mass as you put your mail in your missal, and this is the nearest church—"

She felt a pouring of joy and life, as when she discovered it wasn't the bus that had hit her on Grafton Street, but the flying God-sent body of the jaywalker.

Her voice was shaky. "For a second I thought you were a genie out of a bottle of Dom Pérignon . . ."

"Let's get off these steps and out of Macy's window, have

you had breakfast?" Still holding her hand, he walked her rapidly in the direction of the Royal Hibernian. "Then we'll get you some, I've changed hotels, and I'm going to ask you as a favor not to tell Waldo I'm still here. I haven't made his holidays any happier, but I couldn't go without seeing you alone."

This request and explanation mystified her a little but she was too happy and excited to press it. He was tall and close, beside her, a Christmas morning blessing. Under a soft cold gray sky, the city seemed to be rocking with bells. And Bernard about to be solved— Everything lovely, everything miraculously right, for a little while.

Until Waldo came back from Dunfawny House and the morning moved into the past.

"Just the quickest cup of coffee—I have to rush—" She got out Bernard's note and he read it as they walked. His expression was puzzling: relief like the sun coming out from behind a cloud, and then a frown of doubt.

"Of course you have to go," he said, more to himself than to her. "It has to be settled, one way or another, you can't live with this much longer— Has Waldo seen this?"

"He's off country-house visiting, he won't be back until the afternoon, but he left me the car because his head's still funny."

"Good. I'll drive you."

She made a stab at considering this as they crossed the black and white marble floor of the Royal Hibernian's lobby and went into the Patisserie. As though it would be at all possible to refuse the offer of his company.

"Don't burn your mouth on your coffee."

"I've got to get it down fast. Cy, what if he's watching from a window or something and sees you in the car, it might just send him into another panic . . ."

"When I get the lay of the land I'll get out of the car and loiter discreetly out of sight before you drive up on your white horse, alone. Yes, all right, we're going now, I can feed you later."

While he got the car out of the garage, she scribbled a hasty note at the desk, for Waldo, telling him she was off to meet Bernard but not saying where, in case he took it into his head that it was his duty, if he came back earlier than he'd expected, to follow her.

Both of them were quiet as he concentrated on getting through the holiday traffic, the tall clumsy blue buses, the occasional horse-drawn cart. They cleared suburban Ballsbridge and after a time had to slow again in Dun Laoghaire, where it seemed the entire town was on its way to or from mass, or driving, with an un-American leisure, dawdling as they went, to immense midday family feasts.

In spite of her warm preoccupation with Cy's presence, and her concern about her errand, she found herself charmed with Dun Laoghaire, the long pretty houses painted in cream, in pale blue, and pink, the winter traces of delightful gardens, the bay lapping across the street from the tall shining windows.

Cy stopped the car at a roadside telephone booth. "Have to confirm a reservation," he said, "I won't be a minute." But it was five minutes before he came back. The police had been understandably puzzled by his request.

Waldo had told her that in summer Dublin Bay reminded him a little of the Mediterranean, with its steeply lifting hills above the great sweep of blue. Clean as a whistle, he said, crystal-clear. Flowers growing in sunny rocky walls, romantic houses, the radiant bay seen from airy heights through trees surprisingly exotic, tamarisks, ilexes, an occasional palm, magnolia, persimmon.

Now, with the gray sky pressing lower, rain beginning to hit the windshield, the bay and its circling hills looked lonely and even a little sad. Traffic thinned and all but disappeared.

Cy reached for her hand and found it clenched and cold on the edge of the seat. He pulled the car to the side of the road, stopped it again, and when she said, "What's the matter?" replied, "Nothing, except it's time we had a reunion," and held her in his arms and kissed her, pulling her away from circling fears back to warmth and safety.

"Dear mind-reading Cy . . ." She touched his cheek. "I was just nervously rehearsing my lines . . ."

"We should be almost there," he said, studying Bernard's rough map. "We take a right turn up into the hills at St. Colum's Road, will you watch for it in case I miss it?"

In a few moments she saw the sign. St. Colum's Road, at right angles to the bay road, went up very steeply through a tunnel of beeches. Moss-grown grassy stone walls on either side rose to a height of close to six feet.

"From wherever it is up there, he'd probably be able to see down, although with all these trees I don't know . . ."

Cy looked at the map again. "He has an arrow here, saying one-half, I suppose he means half a mile, before the X for the house or cottage or whatever it is, we're all right for a bit longer."

The narrow road leveled off after the beech tunnel and then heaved itself upward again, this time through a grove of black alders sighing and glistening in the rain.

"I'd better get out here." He took her hand again, in both of his, as if to pass physical strength and calm to her. "Waldo doesn't by any chance keep binoculars in the glove compartment?"

"No . . ." Don't go, don't get out of the car.

Nonsense.

"All right, I'm a country gentleman out for a tramp in the rain." He looked down at his vested Harris tweeds. "Too bad I haven't a pair of gun dogs. But then, he doesn't know me anyway . . . I won't be far behind you. Drive slowly, as you would, hunting an unfamiliar place."

The hand tightened on hers.

"I suppose you know how to scream."

Taking the wheel, watching him move out of sight into the alders, she wished that at the last minute he hadn't looked so suddenly, so terribly worried.

This was her first time driving on the left and she kept, even moving as slowly as she was, wanting to pull over to the other side, convinced that around that sharp curve right up ahead a car would come careening directly at the Mercedes on its wrong side of the road.

A high brick wall, surrounding she supposed the estate, or as the Irish called it the demesne, accompanied her up yet another hill. Hill being too mild a word, these must be the spurs of the Wicklow Mountains.

At the top, the road ended, the wall curved directly in front of her, towering wrought-iron gates wide open, a lane or driveway winding off beyond to be lost in trees. Just inside the gate was a graceful small building of dark gray stone that by its situation proclaimed its identity.

And anyway, this was the end of the road, this had to be Bernard's host's gatehouse.

Its front entrance faced the drive, two stone steps, a door painted yellow, small-paned sparkling windows on either side of it. A large dirty oil-stained motorcycle leaned against the house wall beside the steps.

Not wanting for reasons she couldn't analyze to take the car through the gates, she made a U turn and left it across the road, headed downhill, and got out and walked across the purple macadam and up to the front door.

There was a small note pinned to the door, carelessly printed in pencil. "Gone to Dalkey for milk, right back, key under mat, B."

She was to go in alone, then, into an empty unknown house. Under no circumstances.

But two things changed her mind.

There was a human, bumbling, bachelor inefficiency about Bernard's running out of milk for his coffee, or his tea, just as he prepared to play his final family scene; oddly reassuring.

And if Cy, from some near distance, saw her hesitating, waiting in the rain at the yellow front door, he might think she had taken fright, or heard something alarming inside. He would come to her aid, possibly just as the milk errand was completed. Another confrontation would be aborted, and Bernard would go on forever and ever and ever.

She took the key from under the mat and unlocked the door and went in, mentally whispering her old command to her cowardice.

Cope. *Cope.*

Where were the gatehouse keeper and his wife if he had one? At mass, maybe—

The house was very dark. To the right of the hall was a faded sitting room, small, crowded with furniture, a print of a crimson-robed golden-bearded Christ over the mantelpiece, no Christmas gaieties to be seen, tangled ribbons and bright crumpled wrappings, wreaths or greens.

There was a strong smell of damp, and a creeping cold. It felt as if nobody really lived there, but this could be put down to a lack of self-indulgent central heating. No scent of tea, toast, cabbage, no breath of wax, soap, no rumor of boiling potatoes, nothing.

She went into the sitting room, thought about taking a chair, decided against it, and went to the window looking out on St. Colum's Road and in a sort of game tried to see how well Cy was hiding himself.

Very well indeed. Black dripping trees, a wind picking up the gray and purple skies now, hurling and billowing them. But lovely, to know he wasn't far away, watching. Waiting.

From behind a closed door in the opposite wall from the window came a small sound. A cat. Nice to have another living creature in the house with her.

She pushed the door open and saw the black and white cat in—what was it, a pantry, some kind of storage room?—and was bending to stroke it when there was a whirl of movement behind her, the door was pulled closed, and something soft and thick was whipped around her throat.

Tightening. She arched away in useless power, made a terrible tearing sound, reached back to fight the flesh, the bones, that wanted her death.

A flicker of memory, from the few seconds when there had been light seeping into this blackness, when she had just touched the cat's soft fur, sent her hand to a shelf in front of her, finding blindly and accurately a heavy iron skillet.

She managed to swing it back, hard, over her shoulder. There was an awful crunching thump, a staggering away from her, the crash of a body falling into glass and crockery, the soft noose loosened, dangling.

The merest line of gray light showed her the door at the other end of the pantry.

She stumbled over the cat, which gave out a small shriek of pain, fell against the far door, got through it into a grim little faucet-dripping kitchen, saw another door to the left of the iron sink and as she flung it open and jumped the three steps to the ground heard with the accuracy of the doomed a slow, faintly renewed noise of disheveled glass and broken dishes.

Death collecting itself, getting itself up from the corner or the floor of the pantry.

She thought she knew, refused to know, and in a passion of panic dived and ran through a heavy grove of firs, covering and concealing.

"I suppose you know how to scream . . ."

But if she did, to Cy, and he, the other one—don't name him—was behind her among the streaming boles and entangling branches, she would be placing herself precisely, for him. Here I am, come along and finish it.

Rain blurred her glasses. Incredible that they should still be clinging to her nose.

An ornamental little footbridge lifted itself over a stream. She fled across it, gasping and weeping.

To her left, seen out of focus as from the windows of a fast-moving train, was the drive, with at its end a great cream and black house, the black of it announcing in a faraway voice a ruinous fire.

Like an animal, she kept to the once carefully cultivated wilds of the demesne, a stand of bamboo, an aisle of monkey-puzzle trees, great box hedges around a huge abandoned garden, an old chapel, or folly, in whispering woods, dangerously beckoning.

No, can't take shelter there; cower and wait for what was going to happen, to happen.

But how long would her anguished breathing last her?

Half-clawing, half-climbing her way up a grassy bank under tamarisk trees, hair in her eyes and nothing left to her but some raw surviving center, she found herself exposed again in an open space, bolted through a stone archway onto the drive, running still but fatally tired, with the sound of feet behind her.

Not enough time to turn and see and she didn't want to.

He was catching up with her.

Yes, the end of another road, the end of the long lime-treed drive, which swung to the left to circle the dead house.

And facing her another high brick wall, far beyond her scaling.

There was a great beech tree with low-trailing branches not fifteen feet away.

Cornered, she went back twenty-five years, kicked off her shoes, leaped for a beech branch, pulled herself up into a crotch, swung into the next branch above, and barely able to breathe, completely unable to speak, looked down at Waldo.

CHAPTER 22

In a grotesque attempt at sustaining sanity of a kind, Celia at last managed to speak and asked from her perch, "Did you think I was Bernard—back there in the pantry or whatever it was?"

He leaned in what looked like exhaustion against the tree and gazed up at her, in every way a stranger. Dark knitted cap pulled down to his eyebrows, a web of fresh bright red blood around his nose corners, his mouth, dripping off his chin.

She heard the rasp of his own breathing, as desperate as hers.

Dizzy and holding on hard to the branch above her, she saw again the toe of a gleaming black calf shoe, on Grafton Street, and felt the personal, furious shove, and heard herself saying to tolerant patient Cy,

"Someone tried to kill me."

And on a hillside near Malahide, someone behind her, chasing her, a presence associated with dripping bloody game bags and the sound of guns, and having, that long ago, to run as she thought for her life. Turning out to be only Waldo, trying to catch up with her, trying to . . .

Mrs. Kelly in her glee: "If it had been me, now, in the woods, dark and all, guns around and Kelley here hard behind me, I think he might have seized the golden opportunity of doing away with me, who'd know who was responsible?"

And the man looking for his three-legged beagle, "Ah, sorry, you're in trouble . . ."

While she watched him, the picture to be preserved forever in ice, he took a cigarette from his case, lit it, drew on it, threw it away.

He took off his shoes and his black raincoat, transferring something from the raincoat to his trousers pocket, she couldn't see what, under the covering hand.

Then he reached over his head and lithely pulled himself up into the first, inviting branch, scrambled to his knees on it and reached up for the next.

Where was Cy? Expecting her, connecting her, with the front of the gatehouse, waiting for the yellow door to open, perhaps preparing to storm it if it took too long, opening.

She had no idea whether, running, she had taken a course near the wall, or away from it. Or how long it had taken, or how far, how remotely far, she was, from him.

From distant childhood, her grandmother's voice gave her a piece of advice delivered when in an emergency the Gores were running around in circles. "Make haste slowly."

She climbed again and reached a great angling where she allowed herself several seconds to look down. Waldo was making haste slowly too, graceful about it. The rain, heavy now, made the bark slippery.

In this late mid-morning, there was a twilight darkness, the clouds seeming to press the treetop.

He was moving, underneath, away from her, out on a long heavy limb. She saw what his ascent, his strategy was to be: avoid the immediate encounter, the dangerous savage kick, from a victim momentarily in a place of advantage.

Go around, and above, well out of her reach, and then come down upon her.

She threw back her head and heard, in tune to her scream, an enormous chiming of Christmas bells from some church hidden in a near fold of the hills.

Cy, did you hear me?

The bells died and she screamed again, and moved slowly, laterally out from the secure comforting nook, along a branch roughly opposite to the one Waldo had reached, twenty feet away from her.

If only he would say something, call something to her, no

matter how terrible the words, instead of addressing his capable silent body to the tree.

As she crawled, her knee dislodged a huge bird's nest with a few fragile broken shells in it and sent it plunging to the ground.

Broken things, falling . . .

She judged herself to be about twenty-five or thirty feet above the rough grass.

The most she had jumped as a child had been a daredevil ten, fourteen feet, and that had sent a tremendous shock through the soles of the feet up the body to the thundering head.

She had no weapon; somewhere she had dropped her handbag and her pockets were empty. Even the thin gold compact, to hurl at his head, upset his balance. If only—

She went out as far as she dared before the branch began to bob dangerously under her weight. At no point did any part of the tree touch the brick wall, but now she could see down over the wall into steep empty peaceful meadows, two horses, a faint far glimmer of the bay through the rain.

Her stockings, she noted in a dim objective way, were torn and one foot was bleeding.

She snatched another look over her shoulder. He was higher, now, working back toward the main trunk. Rain ran down his face like tears. There was a long rent in one knee of his dark trousers.

Throw her to the ground? Yes, unless she got there on her own before him.

To the police: Well, you've seen what Caldwell's methods have been, the man's mad. Explaining the sprawled broken body.

And if she did reach the ground, she would run again, if there was any breath left in her body, and he would run, lithe swift Waldo.

Had she stopped screaming? She didn't know.

There was a splitting, cracking noise above her, just as she got a grip of the bark to swing her body down its hazardous stairway.

He dropped through air, caught at and somehow held onto the branch her dangling feet were groping for, and hung there gasping.

Impossible to pull herself back up. But she did, hooking her feet over first, and then her knee, and then half-rolling, half-lifting herself to inch backward toward the trunk. If she didn't reach it, trembling as she was and increasingly dizzy, Waldo need do nothing to her after all.

She would save him the trouble, and fall.

Waldo's dangling, seeking feet found a place to hold him, a place where he could rest and recover strength and breath. Then he too began moving toward the trunk, not even looking up at her.

There was no need. He had her way down blocked. She saw, stuffed into his back pocket . . . something . . . plaid . . . was that what had been around her neck, in the pantry? But now he wouldn't need it.

He reached up and fastened a hard hand around her ankle and began to pull.

She hugged the beech trunk in a last clench of muscle and started screaming again.

There was some kind of movement below them, a voice.

"Let go of her foot, Waldo."

A voice you might use to a child, patient, calming.

She felt inside her own body the thump of Waldo's heart, the sudden stillness in the hand on her flesh.

The same hand on her shoulder, as he kissed her one Christmas morning. "Merry merry, darling . . . don't open a thing until I get back . . ."

Tears and rain almost blinding her, she cawed the name.

"Cy—"

Cy backed away from where he had been standing, close against the foot of the tree, so that now he could be seen, drenched, hair in his eyes, something in his hand, a pointed rock.

"I waited a bit because I didn't know whether you were try-ing to save her or kill her," he said, still in his calm way. "I thought she might be running away from Bernard and that you'd dashed from whatever-it-is house to her rescue. Or set some kind of Caldwell trap here."

Waldo released her ankle and moved away a little. She saw that one of his hands, holding on a foot or so away from her, was bleeding.

"You might as well both come down, you first, Waldo," Cy went on, still soft, controlled. "There's no point in this now, no point at all. You can't go ahead with it in front of a witness, you know. And anyway, Bernard found a friend in Dublin, a woman, she knows all about it, that cap of yours, McGet-tigan's, your meeting with Caldwell and suddenly he's not around any more—"

Waldo reached for his pocket. He took out a gun.

Celia sensed in him a last recklessness and joy and power.

"Which eye would you like to have shot out, the right or the left?" he asked, echoing the conversational tone of the man below.

Without any kind of conscious thought, and giving in at last to her shattering despair, in the tree, his wife abandoned her hold on the trunk, pulled herself to her feet, and dived suicidally down on his body, felt herself in air, and then in great pain, and then nothing.

CHAPTER 23

Blurs, tunnels, gouts of light and sound going away again.

The once calm voice now torn, rasped, with tears in it.

"Oh Christ, oh Christ . . . *Celia* . . ."

Blue legs, official-looking, a lot of them, a torrent of legs.

The unattractive noises of pain, whine tangled with sob, a shriek, "Don't, oh no, don't *touch* me—" and a handkerchief very gently held to her eyes.

". . . he, or rather the two of you, broke her fall but from the looks of him he's broken his neck, the creature—"

After some kind of long lapse, into which penetrated the distressing noises made by fire engines, police cars, or ambulances, the shaken voice again:

"I've seen quarrels that could tear the soul to pieces, but I've never seen a man—physically, lethally—stalk his wife . . ."

Doctorly, plummy voice, "I think you might be able to use a brandy, Mr. Hall."

She connected the syllables with a taste of hot sweet tea that dribbled ignominiously down her chin.

". . . there's a good girl, the other arm's shot, I'll have this one if you please . . ." A light prick, a wasp, a bee, a needle.

"And now let's see . . . wrist and collarbone, man, you're lucky yourself to have—"

Waldo. Back somewhere in time, a wild cry, hanging high in a tree and floating across a brick wall, horses grazing. Mrs. Patrick Campbell saying, It doesn't matter what you do as long as you don't do it in the street and frighten the horses . . .

Like a bystander idly regarding a scene that had no interest or significance to offer, she became aware of hospital corridors, figures in white, the whisper of rubber wheels under her.

After a time another long black tunnel opened and swallowed her.

. . . Voices above her head, soft, speculating.

"Is he her husband then?"

"They have different names . . . but with Americans, and the women activists and all, you never know . . ."

"He's asleep next door, I just gave him a peek."

The mind which had deliberately given itself a rest, a white blanking out, began without a second's warning to function.

She cried out and tried to turn over and bury her head in the pillow and then thought she must still be in the tree, there was a piece of rigid wood at her side—

"Mind your arm," one of the nurses said, steadying her. "It's broken but a grand job of setting, and the several ribs too, but you'll be all one again before you know it."

Watching the mouth working, the tears pouring, the other nurse murmured, "He said he was to be waked instantly if she was frightened or upset—"

The door opened and Cy came into the low lamplight, hair tousled, looking curiously young in his white pajamas and bare feet.

"I'll spend a few minutes with your patient, dear girls," he said. "Suppose you go and fill in charts or something."

Celia looked, appalled, at the bandaging under his collar and around his wrist.

Intercepting her, he said, "Minor breakage, nothing serious. I wouldn't be here at all but I thought you might need me and next door is as close as the law allows."

He pulled a chair to the side of the bed and held her hand very tightly, trying to anchor her in her grief and shock.

"Is he—"

"He's dead, yes," Cy said. "Instantly. Broken neck. And, as the old saw says, very mercifully." Seeing her, motionless but fleeing away, running for her life, he urged, "Love, you're going to have to talk yourself back into . . . sanity. It can't be taken like a pill. And no better place to do it than a hospital bed."

She took her hand away from him, seized paper tissues, and dealt with her eyes, her nose; tears on her chin and down her neck to be blotted.

"And . . . Bernard?"

"The police will be here in the morning, which isn't far off—" He looked at his watch: three o'clock. "They'll take over the search. I think myself he's dead and that he may never be found, he could be under the earth, anywhere, or the sea, it's a lonely landscape here . . ."

"And you think Waldo . . ."

"Yes, say it. Killed him. Up to the last minute, in that tree, I didn't know what was going on, a hunt or a rescue. He might even have bluffed his way out of it—claim he wasn't trying to pull you down, as he was, but steady you, save you. But when I told him about that woman in Dublin knowing all about it, he got his gun out. Gloves off, game over."

He put his head very gently into the hollow between her chin and shoulder. "Which of my eyes did I want shot out . . . ? And you almost committed suicide to save either or both of them, and my life while you were at it."

"That gun." She stared at it, mentally.

He read her mind. "Bernard seems to have been a man to use his hands, on people. I suppose it was a sort of insurance, no slip-ups this time, no matter what."

A whisper into his hair. "Why did he . . ."

"I'll make it short, you want sleep." He told her about John Van Loon's investigations in Philadelphia, and about Bernard's confidences to Doreen, ". . . diamonds . . . silver . . . a regular mint."

"He had, through you, his hands on what sounds somewhat like a fortune and I suppose he saw Bernard as a permanent threat, a maggot digging in. Over and above that, he'd set himself up as the ideal killer for *you*, Waldo elsewhere, clean."

H 38   Talk yourself back into sanity. She caught back a mind in panicked flight, drank water, and said in a low discovering voice,

"He brought me here to kill me. For the house. He tried at least twice and I think three times. He thought . . . knew . . . that we were over one way or another, because of you, and that I'd want a divorce. He asked me"—eyes widening, not seeing Cy at all but the reflections of two people at breakfast in night-dark panes—"where I'd put our wills. Between bites of ham and egg . . . And this time it should really have worked, shouldn't it? I'd have the letter and map on me, I left a note at the desk saying who I was meeting, and now that I think about it, it was Bernard's scarf he had around my neck . . . and then in his pocket . . ."

Rolling her head to one side, away from the impossible truth, plucking at something, anything but what she had just said, "How is it you didn't tell me about that woman— Doreen?"

"Because everything she had to report could be read as plain sloppy straying on his part, or on the other hand as Waldo having dealt with him one way or another. It wouldn't have done to imply to you that there was a possible murderer in the next twin bed, even if I was all that sure of it myself, which of course I wasn't."

He took her hand back. "That business of six months—he probably thought you might bolt, immediately, to me. I almost asked you to, remember?"

"Yes. And he had to keep me long enough to . . ." She closed her eyes.

His voice very far away, he said, "And me convincing myself that he'd do anything to *keep* you, along with . . ."

"Yes, I know. Irena. I was almost happy when the light finally dawned, about her, I thought how nice for everybody."

His hand tightened painfully on hers. He was as close as he could come to severity. "Celia, don't start crying again or you won't be able to stop it."

Lingering a discreet five feet away from the closed door of

the room, one of the nurses said, "They've had a good fifteen minutes, she's to have a sleeping pill, I don't know should I—"

The other said tolerantly, "Hold off for a little, Rose. His collarbone and wrist, her arm and her ribs, bandages and splints between the two of them—sure they can't come to any harm at all."